Identity Theft

by Alana Terry

"For now we see only a reflection as in a mirror; then we shall see face to face. Now I know in part; then I shall know fully, even as I am fully known." 1 Corinthians 13:12

www.alanaterry.com

CHAPTER 1

"Dinner was fabulous." Kurtis flashed that same boyish smile Lacy had grown so used to. "Just like you."

Lacy's lip trembled. She hoped he didn't notice. She tried to meet his eyes. He deserved that much, at least.

"It was awful sweet of you to cook so much." What Kurtis didn't know was how long she had agonized over her recipe books. What kind of meal was appropriate for a night like this?

"Don't mention it." In fact, she hoped he wouldn't.

Kurtis leaned back in his chair. So content. Could she really end things like this? No warning, no explanation …

"So, I've wanted to talk to you about something." Lacy tested her voice. She should have warned him. Should have given him some hint of what was coming. She studied his face, the laugh crinkles around his eyes, the little bit of scruff on his chin, the soft jawline that made him look more like a first-grade teacher instead of a state trooper.

Her gut squeezed up, as if someone had clenched a fist

around her stomach. She could get through this. She had to. It was for Kurtis. It was for the best.

"Daddy! Daddy!" The small, squeaky voice shot a searing pain through Lacy's chest as Madeline rounded the corner and skidded to a stop by the table. "It's skipping again."

Kurtis scooped his daughter up in his lap and nuzzled his nose behind her ear. "My munchkin needs help with the DVD, huh?"

She stuck out her lower lip and pouted. "It skipped."

"Well you know what that means, don't you, Munchkin?" Kurtis winked mischievously at Lacy, who smiled through the gnawing emptiness in her heart. "That means you get to start over from the very beginning."

Once realization set in, Madeline's eyes widened in delight. "Really?"

"You heard me."

She almost jumped off his lap, but then she eyed his plate. "Can I try a bite of fish first?"

He shook his head. "Miss Jo made a special adult dinner tonight. This is just for us."

She pouted and wrinkled her nose. "Does it have peanuts? Is that why I don't get any?"

"No." Kurtis gave Madeline a pat on the bottom and set her

down. "But now go eat your chicken nuggets like a big girl, ok?"

Madeline scurried back down the hall. Kurtis had already changed her into her footed pajamas in case she fell asleep on Lacy's bed. It was the middle of summer, but the mosquitoes were so bad nobody in this part of Alaska dared to wear shorts even indoors.

Lacy watched as Madeline disappeared around the corner. Kurtis stared at the empty hall with a contented expression on his face. Lacy had never known a more attentive father. In fact, until she met Kurtis at the daycare, she had imagined they were mostly figments of overactive imaginations or literary archetypes.

He turned his eyes back on her. Kind eyes. Eyes that would in a moment or two betray sadness, shock, grief. How could she endure the next five minutes? Would he try to change her mind? She had never seen him angry before, not even after her co-worker Kim accidentally gave Madeline a granola bar with peanuts in it at the daycare. Kurtis was away on a domestic violence call when it happened, but when he got back, he assured Kim it was only a mistake. Then, to thank Lacy for her quick use of the EpiPen, he asked her out on their first date.

"This salmon was fabulous," Kurtis declared. "A perfect

dinner." He leaned forward, stroking Lacy's cheek with his finger. "Everything you do is perfect."

If only he knew. If only he realized why Lacy had spent so much time on tonight's meal. In the past four years since she moved to Glennallen, she had learned cooking could be therapeutic to numb her mind from painful memories. It could be utilitarian to provide meals for two dozen daycare kids as cheaply and healthily as possible. Now, she realized cooking could also be a way to say good-bye.

"So, what's the big news?" he asked after taking a sip of sparkling cider. She had thrown it into her cart at Puck's grocery store at the last minute. Now, she regretted it. She regretted inviting Kurtis and Madeline over for dinner. Maybe she should wait. She could call him and tell him by phone. That way she wouldn't have to see his face, didn't have to watch the way his laughing eyes brimmed over with hurt. Betrayal. It would be easier that way, at least for her. Easier if she didn't have to watch him react.

No. She was a grown woman. She couldn't wimp out. She had stalled too long. She had to get it over with. Get on with her life.

"I'm moving." The words fell flat. If she were still involved in theater, any decent director would make her redo that line.

But she couldn't do theater anymore. No drama, no voice lessons, nothing from her former life.

Kurtis set his cider goblet down slowly. Tenderly. He no longer smiled, but his eyes were still so soft. So compassionate. From their first date on, she had known he was the kind of man who would understand. If she had told him everything, he would have found the right words to say. Would have helped carry the loneliness that had been thrust on her four years ago.

"Moving?" He licked his lip. "Wow, that's ... Well, I mean, that sounds like an adventure. When?"

"The end of summer," she answered.

His smile was forced, but it didn't waver. "What are you going to be doing?"

There was a reason she didn't know her plans yet. It was so she couldn't give him any clues. She couldn't have him following after her. Some people used the word *uprooted* to talk about moving. With Lacy, it was more like splattering paints onto a canvas until there was no way to tell what hid beneath all the layers.

She squeezed her eyes shut for a moment. Why had she thought she could get through this? He was right there, with just a foot between them. She could reach out, sob the entire story into his shoulder. He was strong enough to take that burden from her. But she couldn't ask him to. It was impossible.

As impossible as good-bye.

"I might go back to school." It wasn't a lie. She had thought of giving college another try. Had thought about it for the past four years.

He swallowed. "That's ... that's amazing. Good for you. I always told you that you could be anything. Do you know what ..."

"I can't see you anymore." She blurted out the words as fervently as she would have clutched at a life saver if she were drowning in the Copper River. She let the words topple out of her, gaining momentum as they spilled out. She watched her message snowball and take force, gaining speed until full realization punched him in the face.

Kurtis scrunched up his nose. His expression revealed shock, everything except for his eyes. There was no surprise there. No anger. Just the sadness. The incurable hurt of Lacy's betrayal.

"Is it him?" he asked. "Is it Raphael?"

Lacy regretted ever telling Kurtis about him. She should have known better. "No. It has nothing to do with him."

In a way, that was true. But in on the other hand ...

Kurtis took a slow sip of cider. She wanted to jump up

from the table and refill his glass. Anything so she wouldn't have to see his reaction. From down the hall, chipper music from Madeline's movie waltzed uninvited into the dining room.

"I'm sorry," Lacy whispered. If only she could tell him the truth. He would understand. The temptation to reveal everything clung to her limbs, like dead weight in a marshy bog.

He stood up.

"What are you doing?"

He punched buttons on his phone without responding. She wanted to stand, too. Wanted the memory of being with him one last time. Feeling his strong arms surround her. He was a trooper. A protector at heart. She shut her eyes, remembering the feel of their first embrace. Stinging hot memories mingled in her gut, and she wanted to run to him. Forget life had existed before they met.

But she couldn't. Instead, she sat motionless while Kurtis scowled into his phone.

"What are you doing?" she repeated.

He held out his cell. "I want you to see something." His voice was still soft, but there was a restrained tremor behind it. "Do you know what this is?"

Lacy averted her eyes as soon as she saw the picture. This wasn't really happening. This couldn't be happening.

"Do you remember when I went to Anchorage a few weekends ago?"

"I remember."

No. No, this couldn't be. This wasn't real.

"I didn't tell you what I was shopping for." He brought the phone closer to her face. "This is for you. The jeweler is resizing it. I just have to go pick it up."

She shook her head. No. If she could have disappeared by sheer force of will, she would have.

"I love you, Jo." He dropped to his knee in front of her chair, still holding out the screen to show the glistening white gold band in its black velvet case. "I was waiting for the Fourth of July, for the salmon feed. Now hear me out. I know that your mind is set to move, and you know I'd rather die than try to stand in the way of your goals. I'm not going to beg or anything. But listen. I've only got six more months until my placement in Glennallen is up. That's not very long. Then wherever you are, I want you to let me join you. Start a new life together."

A single hot tear slipped down her cheek like melted crayon wax, searing her skin. She didn't wipe it away. How many times could her heart break before it shattered into a pile of shards, never able to heal again?

"I don't need an answer now." He put his hand on her knee. She wanted to grab it, wanted to beg him to whisk her away to an imaginary place where pain from the past could never reach her.

She remained immobile.

"Promise me you'll think about it." He tilted up her chin and gave her a small kiss as he stood. He cleared his throat. "Munchkin!" he shouted down the hall.

Madeline scurried toward them, looking adorably plump and squishable in her pink pajamas. "Time for dessert?" she piped.

Kurtis didn't meet Lacy's gaze, didn't acknowledge her silent pleading. *Forgive me.*

"Give Miss Jo a hug good-night."

Lacy knew the sound of Kurtis's tight voice would haunt her dreams.

"But my movie isn't over," Madeline whined.

"You can watch another one at home," he mumbled. It was enough to mollify his daughter. Madeline spread out her arms so Lacy could pick her up for a hug.

Please forgive me. The words stuck in Lacy's throat. She caught Kurtis's eyes for a fleeting second, recognized the piercing pain that stabbed searing hot into her heart as well.

"Thank you for dinner." He was either braver than she was or a better actor, because he managed a faint smile.

"Wait," Madeline protested. "You haven't kissed her yet."

Kurtis glanced awkwardly at Lacy. Slowly reached his hands out. Lacy's feet steadily closed the distance between them. He wiped her cheek with his thumb and brought his lips close. "Good-bye," he whispered.

She didn't have the breath to answer back.

"That wasn't a very good one," Madeline announced with a pout.

"Come on, Munchkin." Kurtis caught his daughter and swung her into his arms. "Let's go home."

CHAPTER 2

It took half an hour for Lacy to clear the dishes off the table. If she were younger, she would have been surprised she wasn't crying. But she had learned four years ago tears were a luxury that rarely came in the midst of a crisis. They tarried, refusing to let you lose yourself in the bittersweet rush of grief, forcing you to walk through fire with your dry eyes wide open.

Her foster parents would tell her to forgive. She could almost hear Sandy's voice in her mind. *You can hold on to anger, or you can let it go and let God make the best of your situation.* It was a simple premise, really, and it probably worked for good Christian folks like the Lindgrens, folks who took in foster kids and raised them up and helped them graduate high school and saw them through community college. But Sandy would never live through what Lacy had.

It wasn't fair.

She couldn't think of Carl and Sandy, or grief and homesickness would charge at her like an angry moose,

11

knocking her breath out. A tsunami wave far too strong to withstand. Besides, what was the point of dwelling on the Lindgrens? It wasn't as though she would ever see them again.

She hosed herself down with mosquito spray and threw on her shoes. It was almost nine o'clock, but that didn't matter. It never grew fully dark this time of year. She stepped outside, where it was as bright as it had been at noon when she stood out and watched the preschoolers climbing on the daycare jungle gym. At the beginning of summer, she and her co-worker Kim had complained until their boss finally broke down and purchased a propane-operated mosquito trapper. The gizmo was awkward to lug around and cost the daycare five hundred dollars plus gas, but it kept the bugs manageable. Madeline had helped Lacy count the bites on her arm earlier that afternoon.

Only seventeen.

If ever there was a night for ice cream, this was it. Puck's grocery store was only a five-minute walk away. Lacy hardly drove anywhere in the summer except for her monthly four-hour trip to Costco in Anchorage. Lately, she had been tagging along with Kurtis, who was used to driving long distances since he was one of five troopers covering an area the size of Ohio.

Kurtis. Lacy sighed. She hadn't meant to hurt him. She knew it had been a mistake to go on that first date. But it had been winter. She had been lonely. And bored. And if any man could manage to get Lacy to stop aching for Raphael, it was him.

Now she realized she had expected the impossible. What else could she do but cut him loose? He was still young. Good-looking. Rustic enough to appeal to tough Alaska girls, civilized enough to speak to their romantic whimsies. And Madeline ... Over the past few days as Lacy had been preparing tonight's dinner, she had wondered who she would miss more, Kurtis or his daughter who smothered her with kisses and asked Lacy almost every day to become her new mommy.

Lacy hurried through Puck's parking lot, eager to get inside and away from the bugs. Eager for her ice cream. She stopped short when she saw Kurtis through the window. He was pushing Madeline in a cart. She didn't study his expression, didn't try to guess how well he was handling tonight's news. She scurried around the corner without going into the store. One good thing about summer in Glennallen was all the small shops stayed open to cater to the numerous tourists who drove through. She would grab herself an ice cream at the Brain Freeze. She deserved that much, at least. She just hoped she'd make it there before Kurtis came out of the store and spotted her.

She sprinted across the street. She hated running away like

that. Of course, there was no way she could avoid him indefinitely. Glennallen was just too small a town. She was still an East Coast girl at heart, really, fond of the fast pace, the crowded streets, the bright lights, the dazzling skylines. But that life was closed to her now.

She had lost track of how many times she and Raphael had daydreamed about their future. She was finishing up a few classes for her associates and wanted to pursue an undergrad degree in theater. He would set up an art studio in Boston or Cambridge. New York was always their end goal, but for now she wanted to stay near Carl and Sandy, the closest thing she had to family after a childhood spent in and out of foster care. Raphael often told her how proud he was of her, how she had risen above all the negativity in her past to forge a better future for herself. She loved the way he talked to her, the way he encouraged her. She would have never made it to where she was if it weren't for him.

Not that it mattered now, anyway. She couldn't even transfer her credits from the community college. Two years of grueling work had been a total waste. *No use dwelling on the past*, Sandy would tell her. Simple adages, like *Don't cry over spilt milk* that did nothing to address the horror, the loneliness Lacy had lived through. Why was she thinking about Sandy so much lately? If she could just pick up the phone, talk to her. Tell her about Kurtis. But that was impossible, too.

She stepped into the Brain Freeze and glanced around, thankful she didn't see any of the daycare families. She was tired. All she wanted was to forget. Go back in time, never get in the car with Raphael that night.

She ordered a small sundae. It would be about half the size of what she could buy in Anchorage and cost her twice as much, but that was Glennallen for you. People had to pay the heating bills some way. At least the Brain Freeze was bug-free.

Mostly.

She chose a seat by the window and stared outside. Would she see Kurtis's red truck drive by after he left Puck's? Had she really done the right thing? It wasn't fair to him. But did she have any other choice?

A bicyclist spun down the sidewalk. Funny how Alaskans could ride or jog or hike all night long if they wanted and only have to worry about mosquitoes and an occasional grumpy moose. She thought about the weekends when she and Raphael would ride the Boston trails for miles. She let her eyes follow the cyclist. There was something familiar about the way he held himself. Something about his posture …

He glanced up. Their eyes met as he whizzed past her

window.

Raphael?

She whipped her head to follow him. He didn't slow down, didn't look back. It had been her imagination, that's all. A silly mind trick. Even if Raphael were alive, what were the chances …

She couldn't see him anymore. Had he circled around the back parking lot? Had he recognized her, too? How many times had she fantasized about this very moment, bumping into him again after so many years?

Too many years.

Their last night together was supposed to be a celebration. Lacy had just finished her spring semester of community college. Raphael told her it was a big surprise. She didn't admit it to anybody, not even Sandy, but she wondered if this was it. The night he'd propose. They'd talked about it enough, hadn't they?

She didn't know why he brought her so deep into the North End, but she never questioned him. It was a surprise, he told her. The dock he drove toward looked mostly abandoned. It was dark. Nobody was around. It sounded like Raphael's idea of something romantic. Creative Raphael, never content to do anything the traditional way.

"Are you sure you're not lost?" she asked, and he smiled that sideways grin he only got when he was nervous. That's when she knew. This really was it. The Night. She tried to remember every image. Every detail. Then one day when they had a family of her own, she could tell her daughters about the night Daddy asked her to marry him.

Only that's not what happened.

Raphael's whole body tensed behind the wheel the minute the two men appeared. Lacy had been holding his hand, and his fear rushed through his body into hers. "What's going on?" she asked.

"Nothing." He turned off his headlights and reversed the car. "Nothing. I just made a wrong turn."

That's when she saw the body, tied up, struggling. Afterward, she could have sworn she heard the man yelling, but the victim had been gagged and Raphael's car was too far away, so the detective said that was impossible. Still, she heard the sound of muffled pleas even in her dreams, just like she could hear the splash when his murderers dumped his body into the water below.

"Go, go, go," Raphael whispered, coaxing his car. At the time, Lacy still hadn't processed what she had seen. It couldn't be real. Her eyes were playing tricks on her.

"Go, go, go."

Raphael's last words were interrupted by the squeal of tires. He maneuvered the car around and pushed down on the gas. He made it back to the main road before their pursuers caught up. Lacy didn't remember screaming when the gunshot shattered the back window. She sometimes had a vague memory of the airbag exploding into a burst of dust, but she couldn't be certain. Maybe her brain was just trying to fill in the pieces.

She woke up in a dim room, surrounded by three somber police men shooting questions at her as soon as she opened her eyes, pausing only for a moment when a nurse came in to check her vitals.

"Where's Raphael?" Lacy croaked.

The men exchanged awkward looks before one of them declared what she already knew.

"He's dead. I'm terribly sorry, miss."

CHAPTER 3

Lacy thanked the Brain Freeze waitress who brought her the sundae. The ice-cream was ho-hum, definitely not worth the six and a half dollars it cost her. She hated worrying so much about money. She wished Drisklay had given her a different witness protection identity. The daycare couldn't afford to pay her more than minimum wage. The problem was year-round jobs were hard to find in a tourist trap like Glennallen, where weeks straight of negative-thirty temperatures kept all but the hardiest of long-term residents away.

It was the perfect place to hide, really, at least according to the witness protection folks. Four hundred residents, most of whom kept to themselves in typical Alaskan style. She had come in the spring. At least, it was spring in the rest of the world, but here there were still two or more feet of snow on the ground and several weeks of gray mud and gush before it thawed.

It wasn't just the climate she had to get used to. They gave her a whole new name, a new identity. Jo. So brusque, so unfeminine. Sure, she had sometimes wished her birth mom had come up with something unique, something more memorable than plain old Lacy, but Jo? That took longer to get used to than the continual daylight in the summertime or the depressing bleakness of the drawn-out Glennallen winters.

She stared out the window at the place where the bicyclist had disappeared. She knew in her heart it couldn't really be Raphael. The police, the detectives, the press, everyone said he died in the crash. She was left alone. Alone to mourn him in silence. Alone to hide until the two murderers who had chased them went to trial. Alone to testify against the people who wanted her dead.

She thought the witness protection program would be temporary. Detective Drisklay said he'd keep her safe until the trial, and after that she'd be as free as a bird. Then it came out that the murderers boasted a web of Mafia connections. Things got increasingly complicated from there.

Still, she had held on to naïve dreams. Maybe the police knew the Mafia would come after Raphael and helped him fake his death for his own protection. She couldn't get over the impossibly thin thread of hope that he was alive, suffering a trapped, anonymous life in witness protection in some secluded area. She hadn't gathered up the funds or the courage to travel yet, but if she did, maybe she would run into him one day. Reunite at an airport. Catch his eyes on a crowded subway. She couldn't count how many nights she had fallen asleep picturing his face when his eyes met hers. She rehearsed the hug, the kiss, the tears that would mingle on both their cheeks. Crying together over the lost years, vowing to never spend life apart again.

But deep in her heart, she knew her hopes were nothing more than foolishness. Wishful thinking. Impossible dreams she clung to because the pain of reality was too hard to accept.

She stared at her miniature sundae and realized it was melting in front of her while she daydreamed of the past. A perfect metaphor for her life these past four years, really. She picked up her spoon just as the bell on the Brain Freeze door jingled and a new customer stepped in.

She sucked in her breath. Her pulse skyrocketed.

The man walked in, caught Lacy's eye, and gave a shy smile. "Hey, Jo."

She swallowed her disappointment. "Hi, Kurtis."

CHAPTER 4

Madeline ran up to Lacy. "Daddy says I get to have an ice cream because we didn't stay late enough at your house and you didn't even give me any dessert."

Lacy forced a smile. "That was awful nice of him." She avoided Kurtis's gaze.

"Daddy says now I have to be good and promise to sleep in until eight o'clock tomorrow."

"Really? Well I bet a big girl like you can do something like that, can't you?"

She puffed out her chest. "I slept until eight-thirty last Sunday. Daddy was mad because we were late for church, because he promised he would help me make pancakes, but I spilled ..."

"All right, Munchkin," Kurtis interrupted. "You take this ten dollars here and go tell Miss Cathy up at the counter what you want, ok? And be sure to bring back my change."

Madeline's eyes widened. "Can I get a big one this time?"

Kurtis frowned, but his eyes stayed soft. "You know the rules."

Madeline sighed dramatically as she turned around and marched to the counter.

"Mind if I sit down?" Kurtis gestured to the seat. "Or if you'd rather be alone, I can …"

"No, go ahead."

He slipped in the seat across from her.

"I was just …" She took a bite of sundae and didn't bother finishing her thought.

"I'm sorry I left so abruptly." His tone was so kind it plunged icy pangs of guilt into her heart. She should be the one apologizing to him. She regretted so many things. Stringing him on for a year and a half, making him believe she was available. Making him believe her heart still didn't belong to a man who may or may not have been killed in a car crash. The past year and a half with Kurtis had been nothing but lies. She had told him the information Drisklay had spoon-fed her about her past life. That was all. He didn't even know her real name.

"Don't apologize." She resisted the temptation to take hold of his hand which rested between them on the table. *Old habits …*

He took a deep breath. "I've been thinking about it, and I'm sorry if I came across as too forceful. I was just … I was afraid of losing you."

She watched his Adam's apple while he swallowed.

"It's just that after Renee died, I thought I'd never get over it. I thought I'd have to carry that pain around with me my entire life. And I was ok with that, because I had the munchkin. But then I met you, and I was laughing again, and smiling. Madeline told me a few weeks after we started dating that she liked you because you made me act like a good daddy."

Lacy wanted to interrupt, but Kurtis held up his hand.

"You know I love you, Jo. I've already told you how I was going to propose to you at the salmon feed on the Fourth. But I know you've been through a lot, too. You were in a serious relationship, and you lost Raphael just like I lost Renee."

Drisklay hadn't concocted that part of Lacy's backstory. After a few dates, she told Kurtis about a past boyfriend who was killed in a car accident. Looking back, she probably should have changed Raphael's name, but it didn't really matter. Not with someone like Kurtis. The most honest Lacy had ever been with him was when she was talking about Raphael. In a way, the two of them had mourned their lost loves together. The difference was Kurtis had healed.

Lacy hadn't.

Madeline proudly carried her dessert to the table and glanced at her father, who didn't react when she set down a large sundae. She gave Lacy a conspiratorial grin and dug in with her spoon.

"What I'm trying to say," Kurtis continued, "is I'm willing be patient. Whatever it takes, however long you need, I'm willing to wait for you. I want to be with you. But I've been selfish, pushing things when you're not ready. And I want to ask you to forgive me for that. Can we just rewind a few months, start off a little slower? I don't want to scare you away. You're the best thing that's happened to me since ..."

He glanced at his daughter and sighed, letting his words trail off.

Lacy stared at her melting sundae. What had she done to deserve kindness like this? And why couldn't she reciprocate? Was it because of that remotest of possibilities Raphael was still alive? Even if he was, how could she possibly find him? How could she hope to randomly bump into one person out of hundreds of millions?

She knew what she should do. She should accept Kurtis's proposal, or at least keep dating him until she felt ready to take that next step. But her entire identity was a lie. Until she truly learned to embrace her identity as Jo, until she let Lacy die, how could she take such a drastic plunge? It had been a mistake to ever date him in the first place. What if Raphael came back and …

"I'll do it," she blurted.

Kurtis furrowed his brows and looked at her as if she had a fever. "What do you mean?"

"I mean yes. The picture on your phone. Fourth of July. I'm saying yes." She spoke cryptically because she knew Madeline was listening in on every word while she pretended to be absorbed in her ice cream treat.

Madeline's eyes shot up and she looked from Lacy to her dad. "So you're doing it? You're really getting married?"

Lacy figured that with as crowded as the Brain Freeze was combined with how loudly Madeline shouted out the news, every local in Glennallen would hear by the end of the weekend.

Kurtis wrapped his arm around his daughter. "We're having an adult conversation here, Munchkin. I'll tell you all about it when I tuck you in tonight, ok?"

She pouted.

"If you're really good, I'll let you pick out a candy bar before we go, but you can't eat it until tomorrow."

Her eyes brightened, and she took another noisy slurp of

sundae.

Lacy's legs were trembling. Why did they keep it so cold in here?

Kurtis reached out and took her hand in his. "I appreciate that. I really do. And I hope one day you'll let me put that ring on your finger and make things official. But right now, I think you just need time. And I've already promised you as much time as you need." He leaned forward. "I want your whole heart. You know that. I'm not settling for half."

Lacy's lip quivered. "I don't deserve you."

Kurtis didn't seem to hear. "I love you so much. You know that, don't you?"

She nodded.

He glanced at the clock on the wall. "It's getting late, Munchkin. We better go."

"What about my candy bar?"

"On the way out." He sighed and turned to Lacy. "Can I drive you home?"

She had lost her appetite. "Sure." She forced a shaky smile. "Thanks."

They didn't speak on the drive back to Lacy's apartment. It was an awkward two minutes, and Lacy kept trying to think of a way to break the silence. She replayed their conversation in her mind. Were they engaged? Had they broken up? Why were things so confusing? If she really was Jo, she would marry Kurtis in a heartbeat. He was an attentive boyfriend, a caring father, and he had raised a terrific kid. He was the perfect match for someone like Jo, a small-town daycare worker living a simple life in rural Alaska. No debt, no student loans, no real ambitions. That's the life Jo was made for.

But as hard as she had tried to seize her new identity, Lacy still wasn't Jo. Tonight of all nights, it seemed she never would be. She was an East Coast girl. A theater aficionado. All but engaged to an up-and-coming contemporary artist who loved her wildly. Passionately. With Raphael, she had felt exhilarated. Terrified. Excited. Overwhelmed, all at the same time by his zeal and ardor. Life with him was like sky-diving. One thrill after another, peaks of adrenaline, new adventures — spontaneous adventures — every day. She couldn't even guess how many miles they had put on Raphael's air-brushed Saab, driving from one art show to another. Life with Raphael was like the East Coast itself. Fast-paced. Vibrant. Colorful.

And Kurtis? With Kurtis, Lacy felt safe. Safer than she had ever felt in her entire life, actually. With Kurtis, she felt cherished and protected and adored. But there wasn't much difference between feeling adored and feeling smothered.

Still, she should try. She should try to patch things up with Kurtis. There were worse fates than ending up with someone safe. Besides, if the Mafia ever did catch wind of where Drisklay had stashed her away out here in the middle of nowhere, it wouldn't hurt to be married to a state trooper with a whole arsenal of guns in his personal collection.

Kurtis pulled up in front of Lacy's apartment. "I'd walk you in, but it looks like the munchkin is about to fall asleep."

"I'm not asleep," Madeline protested through a yawn.

Kurtis passed his phone to the backseat. "Here, find the pictures of you and Grandma at Disneyland last year. Look through those while I say good-night to Miss Jo."

Madeline didn't protest, and Kurtis leaned toward Lacy. "You know I'll always care for you, right?"

Why did he say it that way? Why didn't he say he loved her like normal? She imagined responding that she loved him too, but the words caught in her throat.

"I'm gonna let you go now." His voice was so quiet. What was he saying? Was he saying he was dropping her off for the night? Or was there more to it? More than Lacy was ready to admit right now?

He cupped her cheek with his hand and pulled her face closer. Slowly. Tenderly. As if they both had all the time in the world. His lips met hers a centimeter at a time. Warm. Soft. Just like his embrace. Strong. She sucked in her breath. She wanted to keep him here with her forever. What was wrong with feeling safe? Why had she ever complained about that? She pressed her hand against the back of his head right as he pulled away. His eyes bored into hers. An expression that spoke such tenderness, such bittersweet longing.

"Good-bye, Jo," he whispered.

She opened the truck door, forbidding herself from crying. There would be time for that later. A hot bath, a long cry, and a full night's sleep. She didn't look behind when she heard Kurtis's truck pull away. She knew when she went into the witness protection program her entire life would change, but she had no idea how heart-wrenching the process would be. Four years later, she was still a mess, still grieving Raphael, mourning her lost life. Still wishing she could be Lacy again.

She sighed as she entered her apartment. She never bothered locking her door. That was one Glennallen habit she had picked up right away. Drisklay would probably force her to sit through an hour-long rant if he knew, but this one small act of defiance encouraged her. A small trace of the carefree, rebellious Lacy still remained.

She didn't see him sitting at the dining room table until she was only three feet away. She screamed.

"Lacy? It's me."

Blood drained from her face. She reached out for something to hold onto for balance.

"Raphael?"

CHAPTER 5

Her body couldn't do anything but stare. She had rehearsed this very second so many times since Drisklay and his team relocated her up here. She had imagined how it would feel, the initial surprise, then the shock giving way to euphoria. She had pictured herself running to him, envisioned that first embrace spanning so many tumultuous years. The pain would wash away like marker lines on a dry-erase board.

Instead, she froze in the middle of her own apartment.

He stood. He looked different. Older. Had she aged that much, too? How could she tell? Drisklay hadn't allowed her to take any photographs with her. Too dangerous.

"What are you doing here?" Her breath came in shallow spurts. "How did you find me?"

He ran his fingers through his hair. Glanced around nervously. Let out a chuckle. "Ever since the accident, I've been dreaming of this day. Praying I would find you." He laughed again. The sound was out of place. "I think the only word to call it is a miracle."

She squinted. Was it some sort of hallucination? His face was older, with lines across his brow she had never seen before. His chin was puffier, as if he had put on excess weight, but his voice was the same. Her eyes might deceive her, but her ears couldn't. "It's really you?" She hardly dared to breathe, as if a hard exhale might blow him away into vapor. She still hadn't taken a step closer.

"I was wondering the same thing." His eyes lit up with dancing joy. "I was riding along the Glenn, and I was thinking about something nice and cold to drink, wondering what that ice cream place had, and I looked in the window, and it was you. I tried to blow it off. My mind's played that trick on me dozens of times. But I came back around, and it really was you. I was sure of it."

She heard his words but was unable to string them together coherently in her mind. "How did you get here?"

"Well, I watched for a minute and knew I was either going to make a huge fool of myself or else I was going to always wonder if God really had answered my prayers after all these years. I had already told him if you were with someone else, if you had found someone nice to settle down with, then I didn't want to stand in the way. You know, *Thou shalt not covet thy neighbor's wife* and all that stuff. But then this girl was walking down the road, and I asked her if she lived here, and when she said she did, I pointed through the window and asked if she knew you. And she said, 'Oh, yeah, that's Jo. We work together at the daycare.' So I told her I was your brother and that I was here to surprise you for your birthday but I forgot my phone where I had written your address. So she pointed me to your apartment. And I took a chance sounding stupid, but I asked her if you had a roommate or anything, and she said no, you lived there alone. And well, I'm telling you it took me forever to make up my mind. I could have just left you a letter or something, and I nearly did, but then I started to worry that maybe it wasn't really you. Or maybe you had moved on and I'd spend the rest of my life wondering if you got my note or if there had somehow been some mistake. And I prayed, and I really felt God speaking to me, like he was saying, *Son, you've been asking for me to bring her back into your life for these four years, so what's the problem? Don't you trust me to take care of the details?*"

He was winded from his speech. His eyes sparkled, but Lacy knew him well enough to detect the nervousness behind all that excitement. Even now, she longed to run to him, to forget the trauma of the past four years. Instead, she could only manage saying, "You're in Alaska?"

"Just visiting," he answered. His eyes darted around her room.

She felt naked. Exposed.

"I decided to take the summer off to bike around the country, and I thought to myself, *I've never been to Alaska. I should get on that.* I'm coming back from two weeks up and down the Richardson. Biked from Tok all the way to Fairbanks. I'm on my last stretch now. Heading back to Anchorage tomorrow."

"You're leaving?" She heard her own voice quiver.

He stepped forward. She waited. Expectant. He came up slowly. Took her clammy hand in his.

"I thought you were dead," she whispered.

"It's a long story. Right now, I just want to look at you. I can't tell you how long I've dreamed of this day. I never really thought …" He swallowed. "I'm not sure I ever believed in miracles until now."

"You're religious," was all she could think to say.

"So much has changed these past four years. So much." He brought her hand close to his face as if he might kiss it. He leveled his eyes. "But one thing is the same. I have never stopped loving you."

She pried her hand away, wondering how different this meeting would be if she were wearing Kurtis's engagement ring.

Raphael gave a little chuckle. "I know it's insane. Really, I do. If I hadn't given my life to Christ and had faith that he can do the impossible, I wouldn't have believed it myself. Look, I know you're a little freaked out. And we have a lot of ground to cover. I just … I've been waiting for you for the past four years. And now that I've found you, it's like I want to sweep you up in my arms and transport us back to four years ago and never drive down that …" He cut himself off short and started over. "Transport us back to when we were happy. Happy and young and madly in love and dreaming those crazy dreams for our future. Remember? We were going to backpack Europe and visit all the art museums and come home to our studio and spend our weekends watching shows on Broadway. Just me and my Lacy."

It wasn't until he said her name that she started to tremble. Nobody had called her Lacy in four years. Even when Drisklay telephoned to check up on her, he insisted on using her alias.

Raphael put both arms on her shoulders, as if that could stop her shaking. She was crying, his voice, his touch releasing a tidal wave of pent-up emotions and forgotten longings.

"I need to sit down."

He held her elbow and led her to the dining room table, where Kurtis had proposed to her less than two hours earlier.

"Do you need a drink?"

She nodded faintly, hardly able to focus on his eyes anymore. He opened her fridge, pulled out the goblet of leftover cider. "Is this still good?" Without waiting for an answer, he poured it into a clean cup from the dishwasher and handed it to her. The drink stung her sinuses, but at least it cleared her dizziness.

"I guess I gave you quite a shock." He smiled, that same mischievous grin she had fallen in love with another lifetime ago.

Finally she found her voice. "I just can't believe it's really you. I thought …"

"You thought I was dead, right? Thought they killed me and dragged off my body to the wharf?"

She nodded. "But I still hoped …" She didn't have the strength to finish her sentence. Why couldn't Raphael have visited Glennallen sooner? Why couldn't she had bumped into him her first summer in this rat hole? If there really was a God, and if he really had led Raphael to her after all these years, why couldn't he have done it way back then?

He sat down across from her. "There's so much we have to catch up on. I don't even know where to start."

Neither did she. Part of her was afraid she would wake up and realize this was all a dream, her mind's way of running away from Kurtis after he proposed to her earlier.

"So you're working at a daycare?"

She nodded, the motion inviting another wave of dizziness.

"Do you like it?"

"It's ok." She didn't want to talk about her job, the dirty diapers, dirty dishes, dirty noses that always needed wiping. She should tell him about Kurtis. She should mention it before …

"Alaska, huh? It's pretty up here, isn't it?"

"Yeah." She took another sip of cider, wincing as the fizz burned her throat.

"Your hair's longer."

"Uh-huh." As soon as she moved up here with her short pixie cut, she started growing it out to protect herself from the cold in the winter and the bugs in the summer.

"Jo, they call you, right?"

She stared at her half-empty cup.

He frowned. "You don't look like a Jo to me."

She should say something. Do something. How many times had she dreamed of sitting across from Raphael, pouring out her heart, telling him everything about the past four years of loneliness and isolation?

"Are you happy?" He asked the question so casually, but it punched her straight in the gut.

"Not really." It felt strange to not have to make up lies, not have to spew out rehearsed lines handed to her by the folks at witness protection.

He put his hand on the table but stopped before touching hers. "I've missed you."

"I've missed you, too." It was probably the most honest statement she had made in the past four years.

"Do you want to talk about it?"

Her eyes threatened to brim over again. "Not really." She forced a laugh. She hardly knew how to act like herself anymore. One day, she hoped she could look back on tonight and enjoy a full, long belly laugh.

Raphael sat back in his seat. "How about I do the talking then?"

She nodded, the heaviness already lifting from her shoulders a small bit at a time.

He ran his fingers through his hair. "Wow, this is harder than I thought. I don't even know where to start. At the beginning, I guess. You want me to tell you about the accident?"

"No." She hadn't realized her voice would sound that forceful.

He fidgeted with his hands. Artist's hands. Hands that were always painting or sculpting or photographing. She had missed them so much.

"Well, after everything that went down, they put me in witness protection. Same sort of thing as you, I'm assuming. New home, new name. It sucked. They had me working as a courier. Driving around some hunky-dunk Midwest town running deliveries for divorce lawyers and grumpy realtors. I hated it. Couldn't meet anybody, couldn't go anywhere. They even told me to stop my art."

"Really?"

He nodded. "Of course, I didn't listen. I sold a few photographs under a made-up name, but it was terrible. I'd spent the past eight years of my life building my portfolio, expanding my network. And now they wanted me to start over from the beginning peddling photographs at craft bazaars? I got low. Really low. It was like I was an actor and the producer just threw me into a different play, different setting, different lines, different cast, and no direction."

Lacy wondered how many times she had used a similar

analogy.

"Figured my only outlet was gonna be my art. So I went back to it for real. At first, I tried to disguise it. Make sure someone with a trained eye couldn't link it to me. The old me. Do you know how hard it is trying to paint like someone else? It didn't work. So finally, I decided if I couldn't be a professional anymore, I'd at least paint for myself. Who knew? Maybe one day they'd tell me I didn't have to be in witness protection anymore, and I'd have enough works to sell to set me up for a lifetime. You could always hope, right?"

Hope. It had been one of Lacy's worst enemies during her first few months here in Alaska. Hope that it had all been some sort of nightmare. Hope that Drisklay would call and tell her it was safe to go home. Hope that Raphael would show up magically. Unexpectedly.

"Anyway, I got so depressed I actually ended up … well, they put me in a hospital. Made me talk to a shrink and everything. But what can you tell a shrink, you know? When you're supposed to be someone else, I mean. But one thing I talked about was being homesick. And the hospital psychologist, she had no idea who I was or where I was really from, but she made me write a list of why I should or shouldn't move back home. And I realized the only thing keeping me away from Massachusetts was fear. I mean, can you believe it? You knew me, Lace. I wasn't scared of anything.

"So I started to think. It made sense to keep my new name and whatnot, maybe not hang out in the exact same circles as before. But how bad could it really be, you know? The guys who'd given me the hardest time were both in jail. I suppose they might have had buddies or something ready to teach me a lesson, but what was I gonna do? Spend the rest of my life shuttling divorce papers around town? I moved back about a year ago. I'm living in Waltham now. Best choice I ever made."

"And nobody's bothered you?" Lacy asked. Was it really that simple? Could she really move back home, resume her old life just like that? After all of Drisklay's dire warnings and morbid projections about what would happen if she ever returned? Was it really as easy as Raphael said?

He glanced around. "I started going to church. I guess that's the one good thing that came out of everything. And I figured if God wants me to live, well, I'm going to live. And if not, at least I know where I'm headed, right?"

Lacy hadn't thought about God much in the past four years, unless it was to blame him for letting her life take the unfortunate twists and turns it had. This was a new side of Raphael she wasn't sure if she was comfortable with or not.

42

"Oh!" He smiled and leaned forward, eyes twinkling. "You'll get a kick out of this. I've been going to Carl and Sandy's church."

"My foster parents?"

"Yeah." He sighed. "I wish you could connect with them again. I know they miss you."

Her throat constricted. She had lost hours of sleep since moving to Glennallen trying to recall the exact sound of Sandy's voice. With Carl it was easier, because if she wanted to she could download his sermons and listen to his confident, booming preaching at any time. But Sandy …

"That's neat you get to see them still."

It wasn't fair. If Massachusetts was safe enough for him, wasn't it safe enough for her? She could have moved back years ago, forgotten the blasted mosquitoes, the unbearable winters that dragged out over half the year.

"You could come with me." He stared so intently into her eyes she didn't know whether to laugh or cry or run away. "We could be safe together."

No. No, this was happening too fast. It reminded her of swimming in the ocean once as a little girl when the undercurrent caught her in its black, deathly grasp. It tumbled her over so many times she didn't know which way to turn to get to shore. For a few paralyzing seconds, she didn't even know which way would lead her to the surface. To air.

Her cup of cider trembled in her hand, and Raphael picked it up and set it on the table for her. "I'm sorry. I wasn't trying to upset you."

"I'm seeing someone." The words rushed out automatically.

He didn't speak right away, and she did what she could to fill the silence.

"He's a trooper. We've been dating for over a year now. He has a little girl. She's four." Why was she saying all of this? Was it because she was afraid she might tell him about the ring, about the proposal, so instead she cluttered the empty space with trivia?

Raphael licked his lower lip. He picked up Lacy's cider cup, examined it mindlessly, and set it down again. "I'm glad you told me." He forced a little smile. "I guess I shouldn't have barged in here like this, and ..." He tousled his hair in both hands. "You must think I've been totally insensitive. I'm sorry, Lace."

She couldn't meet his eyes.

Raphael made a move as if to stand up and stopped. "Is it serious?"

She shrugged. "I don't really know right now. It's confusing."

He glanced at the door. "Do you want me to leave?"

It wasn't fair. After all the waiting, all the loneliness, the fruitless fantasizing, now here he was, and she didn't know what to say. "I'm pretty overwhelmed, that's all."

He sighed. "I should have been more thoughtful. Geeze, Lace, you've been through so much already. I don't want to make this harder for you. I listen to my Bible when I ride, you know. I've got it on audio, and just today I was reading about John the Baptist and how he says about Jesus, *He must become greater, and I must become less.* Maybe that was a message for me. I don't want to stand in the way of a good thing. If God's brought you someone who's honest and solid and who'll take care of you ..."

She never knew why she did it. She just couldn't stand listening to him talking like that anymore. She had to make him stop. Either that, or he would do the noble thing and leave her to enjoy some sort of peaceful, lulling happily ever after with Kurtis. She bent forward and kissed him. He sucked in his breath while his lips met hers, and then he wrapped his arms around her, entwined his fingers in her hair. He tasted just like she remembered. If she had a thousand words, she could never express how much she had missed this.

They fell apart, both panting. "Wow." He rubbed his head and repeated, "Wow."

She scooted her chair back, afraid of the feelings his kiss had awakened. "I shouldn't have done that."

"Maybe not." He grinned. "But I'm sure glad you did."

"I can't ..." She held up her hands. "I shouldn't be ..."

He stood. "I understand. It's, well, I can guess it's pretty complicated."

She lowered her eyes. "Yeah." Heat rushed across her face.

"But it was nice, wasn't it?"

She wiped her mouth self-consciously. "Yeah."

"Really nice." Why was he looking at her like that? Didn't he know how irresistible he was? He took a few steps toward the door. "I should go, shouldn't I?"

She should stop him. Keep him here forever. Once she explained everything to Kurtis, he'd understand ...

"Do you mean *go* go?" Her voice squeaked a little.

He paused with his hand on the doorknob. "Is that what you want me to do?"

"No, I ..." She took in a deep breath, trying to clear her mind, which was still racing after the feel of his lips pressed hungrily against hers. "I ... I need time to think. It's nothing personal."

"No problem. I'll give you my number."

She fumbled for her phone in her purse, thankful for something to occupy her hands. She kept her eyes on the screen and typed in his name. "All right, I'm ready."

He rattled off the number. Her fingers trembled a little when she punched them into her cell. What if she got it wrong? What if he went to Anchorage tomorrow and she never saw him again? Maybe she should leave with him. Maybe she should just ...

"I don't fly out until Monday. There's time."

She nodded, eager to get him out of her apartment, searching for an excuse to make him stay.

"It's going to be all right. You know that, right?" He touched her gently on the shoulder, and she tried not to jerk her arm away. This was Raphael. Not the phantom she had dreamed about, pined after for so many years. He was really here, the warm sweetness of his kiss no longer just a bittersweet memory but fresh on her lips.

He bent his head down and kissed the top of her head. "I'll be waiting for your call. If you're happy here, I wish you both all the best. You know that, right? And if you decide you want to come back, well, like I said, I'm driving to Anchorage tomorrow." He glanced at her, his eyes hopeful.

She couldn't speak. She could scarcely breathe. It felt as if someone had stabbed her in the heart and her blood was spilling out in a puddle on the floor.

He held up his phone. "Just call me either way, ok? Even if it's just to say no thanks. I really ..." He cleared his throat. "I really don't want to go another four years wondering, you know?"

She bit her lip.

"Hey, you've still got a Bible, right?"

"Yeah." Drisklay hadn't let her take the one Carl and Sandy signed for her high school graduation, but she found a freebie at the Glennallen thrift store and brought it home, even though she had only opened it once or twice since then.

"Look up Jeremiah 29:11, all right? It's one of my favorites."

She nodded, hardly able to lift her hand to wave good-bye as he walked out of her apartment.

CHAPTER 6

She stared at the door for several minutes after he left. She didn't want to go digging for her thrift store Bible, so she opened up a Scripture website on her phone. What verse had he said? Jeremiah 29:11. It had been so long since she and Sandy had read the Bible together over milk and cookies at the Lindgrens' dining room table. She couldn't even remember which testament she should look in. Thankfully, the webpage made that part easy enough for her. Her phone took some time to load, and she glanced around her apartment. Other than the cup of cider on the table, was there any proof Raphael had been there? She glanced at her cell, wondering if his name and number would be there in her contacts list if she were to look it up.

Jeremiah 29:11. The verse finished loading. She read it slowly. *"For I know the plans I have for you," declares the Lord, "plans to prosper you and not to harm you, plans to give you hope and a future."*

A future? What kind of a future was there for her as long as she stayed in witness protection? A future away from Carl and Sandy, the only parental figures who had ever really loved her. A future in Glennallen, a town with absolutely nothing going for it except for the fact that it was remote and catered to tourists in the summer. A future working at the daycare until she lost every ounce of patience with the children and was forced to quit. And then what? Getting a job at Puck's grocery store? Bagging canned goods and stocking shelves the rest of her life?

Hope and a future. Until tonight, Lacy hadn't really allowed herself to hope for anything besides a mild winter. There was Kurtis, of course, and his proposal. Just a little bit ago, she had all but thrown herself at him, begging him to ignore her initial rejection. But he knew she hadn't meant it. Not really. And now, if he found out about Raphael …

The sting of that last kiss burned her lips. Shame congealed in her veins. What had she been thinking? How would Kurtis feel if he found out?

She glanced at the verse on her screen once more. *"For I know the plans I have for you."* Well, at least somebody did. She was embarrassed to think about how thoroughly she had turned her back on God since she moved here. When she first got to Glennallen, she had gone to the chapel because she missed Carl and Sandy and thought being in a church on Sunday might assuage a little bit of her homesickness. But she got bored. She was tired after working long hours at the daycare. She went back to the chapel when she started dating Kurtis because it was important to him, but other than that hour and a half on Sunday mornings, she rarely thought about the Lord.

How many times had she gone over that evening with Raphael? They could have gone to any pier in North End. They could have dined at any restaurant across the entire Boston-Cambridge area. Why there? Why then? And if God really had a plan for her life, couldn't he have stopped them?

Well, what if that verse was right? What if witnessing the murder on the pier really was part of God's plan? That meant he wanted her in Glennallen. He wanted her to suffer the loneliness, the heartache. Why? So she could meet Kurtis? Then why had he thrown Raphael back into her path?

And if God wanted her to marry Raphael, why had they been separated for these past four years? Even if the Lord wanted to grant them a dramatic reunion after all they had been through, why didn't he stop Kurtis from coming into the picture, complicating everything with his patient understanding?

The phone was heavy in her hand. It was too much to think about tonight. Yet again, she felt that God must be punishing her for some horrible thing she had done in the past. And if he was God, that was probably his right. But why were there people worse than she, people who beat their children or were strung out on drugs, whose lives weren't thrown into chaos? She never doubted God's existence, not really. But it made so much more sense to think of him as a benign being in some far-away universe, too busy to care about the day-to-day affairs of an East Coast foster girl.

Too busy to intervene when Lacy needed him the most.

Well, the answers weren't going to magically appear on her phone. She closed the Bible website and stared at the screen. Should she call someone? Who? Raphael had just left. She could call him now, ask him to take her away with him to Anchorage. Go back with him to Massachusetts. In a day or two, she could be home with Carl and Sandy.

But where would that leave Kurtis? At least his wife was really dead. Renee had died in the hospital. He had seen her buried. He hadn't lived the past several years wondering, dealing with the nagging suspicion, the spark of hope that was almost too painful to acknowledge. But what if she was magically found to be alive? Wouldn't it be his right to dump Jo and spend the rest of his life with his first love?

She should call Kurtis. He was so level-headed. So thoughtful. Even just talking through things with him would help. But to do that would mean revealing her past. What would he say when he learned her entire identity was a fabrication? Somewhere in his vast reserves of compassion, there must be an end to his patience and forgiveness. If he found out the truth, if he found out she wasn't a foster kid from Michigan who moved out to Alaska to fulfill a lifelong dream, what would he say? What would he say if he discovered she hated the cold, hated mosquitoes, hated the claustrophobic, isolated feeling that came from living in a town of four hundred?

What would he say if she told him that she was in love with Raphael? That she had never stopped loving him? That she had known deep in her heart he was still alive even while she was dating someone else? Kurtis was a saint. But she couldn't expect him to sympathize with that. And if he did, if he looked at her with those tender eyes and told her he understood and forgave her anyway, she would feel even more wretched.

Why had Raphael come? Why had they ever gone to that pier in the first place?

"For I know the plans I have for you."

Well, that was all fine and good and poetic, and Lacy

figured that people like her foster mom Sandy would read a verse like that and derive a great deal of comfort from it. But it only made Lacy feel worse. If God had a plan for her, that meant he wanted her in witness protection. He wanted to ruin her life. And then, just because he was all-powerful and just because he could, he was going to throw Raphael at her right after Kurtis proposed.

Some plan.

She shut off her phone. It was late. The sky was still bright enough you could drive without headlights even though midnight was less than an hour away. She plodded to her room without bothering to brush her teeth or change into her pajamas. She closed her curtains, but the light still spilled in through the sides. She plopped onto her bed and threw the pillow over her face. Two mosquitoes buzzed in her ear.

Alaska sucks.

She rolled onto her side and tried to sleep.

CHAPTER 7

She woke up the next morning with at least four new bites. One was on her ankle, the most annoying spot of all. It was a little after eight, and she wondered if she'd be lucky enough to go back to sleep. She was still exhausted. She had lain awake half the night listening to the bugs and trying to organize her thoughts. God might have plans for her future like Raphael's verse suggested, but it had taken her until two in the morning to come up with any plans for herself.

She just hoped she wouldn't regret them.

She flipped on her phone. There was already a text message from Raphael. *Breakfast this morning?*

She wasn't going to think about the shock of seeing him again. She wasn't going to think about the fire that burned in her gut when they had kissed after so many years. *Gotta do something first*, she replied. *Lunch instead?*

Today might be the hardest day of her life.

As she dressed, she thought about calling Kurtis

beforehand. Warn him she was coming. But she couldn't bring herself to do it. If she got him on the phone, the temptation would be too strong to tell him everything she needed to say without looking at him. She couldn't do that to him. She had made up her mind and had the bags under her eyes to prove it. She would never forgive herself if she took the easy way out now.

It took fifteen minutes to walk to Kurtis's house, which helped clear her mind. Her heart pounded faster than normal by the time she arrived, but her limbs weren't as jittery as when she first started out. A slight breeze had kept most of the mosquitoes at bay. When she had made up her mind last night, she pictured walking to Kurtis's in a rainstorm or getting swarmed by a hundred bugs at once, but the trip itself had been surprisingly calming.

She knocked on the door, feeling more like Lacy and less like Jo than she had in years. Lacy wasn't afraid of change. Lacy wasn't afraid to tackle life head-on no matter what the cost. The only thing Lacy feared was a cage, a cage that after today would no longer confine her.

Madeline answered the door, still in her footy pajamas. "Miss Jo!" Her excited squeal sent a pang of regret through Lacy's heart. What had she expected? She knew how hard this would be. It didn't matter, though, she reminded herself. It had to be done.

"Hi, sweetie." Lacy pried Madeline off her leg. "Can you tell your daddy I'm here?"

Madeline scurried away yelling, and Lacy stepped in and shut the door to keep the bugs out. Kurtis came out a moment later in flannel lounge pants and a white undershirt, drying his hair with a towel. "Hi, Jo."

She couldn't tell from his voice if he was happy to see her or not, but she couldn't focus on that. She would say what she came here to say, and that would be all. She was about to apologize for stopping by unannounced, but that was Jo talking, Jo the demure daycare worker who had never really existed. She glanced around the house, at the moose antlers on the wall, the plastic pink princess toys strewn across the floor. She hadn't admitted until now how much she would miss all this.

"I came here to talk to you. Do you have a minute?"

He looked at her quizzically before leaning down to Madeline. "Why don't you grab a Pop Tart and run downstairs to watch some cartoons? I'll make us pancakes in a little bit."

"Is Miss Jo eating with us, too?" she asked.

"I don't know."

Kurtis avoided meeting Lacy's eyes as Madeline skipped

downstairs. He pointed to the couch. "Have a seat." He took the lounge chair opposite her.

Lacy had already decided not to waste time on chitchat. What was the point? "I'm heading to Anchorage. I came to say good-bye."

His expression didn't change. Where was the kindness, the compassion she had grown to expect from him?

She rushed to fill the silence. "It doesn't have anything to do with you. I want you to know that. You're a … well, you're an amazing guy, and I'm really thankful I got to know you." She couldn't read him. Was he angry? "I just, well, I'm leaving, and I didn't want it to come across like I was running away or anything …"

Who was she fooling? That's exactly what she was doing. No, that wasn't it either. She was embracing her own life for a change. Making her own plans.

Kurtis continued to stare.

"Why don't you say something?" she finally asked.

"When are you leaving?"

"Today. As soon as I get packed."

"It was Raphael, wasn't it?" His voice was so soft, she leaned forward to make sure she heard him. "At your apartment last night."

"Ra …" The word caught in her throat. "My apartment?"

"I went back, you know. Went back to tell you I didn't mean it. Went back to tell you that even though the nice-guy thing to do is wait until you're good and ready, the truth is I'm dying inside. I want to be with you. I know last night I said I would wait because I want your whole heart, but it was a lie. I said that for you, because I thought you needed space to sort your life out. But I want you now. I want you here with me, wearing my ring, using my name, raising my daughter with me. I came last night to tell you I couldn't stand the thought of waiting anymore. It was killing me. That's when I saw him leave your place."

Her stomach dropped. "It wasn't what you're thinking. It wasn't …" She stopped short at the memory of Raphael's kiss. She couldn't lie anymore. "It was Raphael. You're right about that. But it's not like I was seeing you both at the same time. Until yesterday I thought he was dead."

"In witness protection, you mean." The words came out flat.

Nervous energy raced up Lacy's spine. "What are you talking about?"

Kurtis let out his breath. "I'm a simple guy, Jo, but I'm not stupid. I know what happened to you."

"What?" She felt like a parrot with a one-word vocabulary.

"Listen, you told me about Raphael. You told me he was killed in a car accident. You gave me the name of your foster parents. You think I couldn't figure it out?"

"But I never told you where I lived."

"No. You did the smart thing and kept that a secret from me. But how many Carls do you think there are who take in foster kids and pastor a church and are married to a woman named Sandy?"

She didn't know what to say. She had never heard him speak like this. "Are you angry?"

"Angry?" He raised his voice. "Geeze. Do you think that little of me? Of course you had to lie to me. Of course you had to keep the past tucked away. If I were mad about something like that …"

"Then why are you yelling?"

He paused to take a breath. "I didn't mean to. But you can't understand that I'm on your team here. I've known about this for weeks. Want to know when I put it all together? When I tried to find Carl so I could ask him for your hand in marriage. And I didn't find a Pastor Carl and Sandy in Michigan where I was looking, but I found them in Massachusetts. So I called. Asked if he had a foster daughter named Jo. He said he and his wife had a lot of foster kids over the years, but nobody by that name. I said she moved to Alaska four years ago. He turned evasive and finally hung up. You think after a decade as a trooper I can't smell suspicious? So I started searching more. Looking up Raphael, trying to figure out how he died. And guess what? He wasn't alone in the car. There was a girl there. A girl your age who testified in court and then disappeared. You think I can't put things together? So then I start to think, the girl got put in witness protection. What about the boy? What if his death's just a cover-up, too? And then I realize why you're having a harder time moving on than I did when Renee passed. You're holding onto hope that he's still out there, that maybe one day you'll find each other, live out your happily ever …"

"I'm not going to Anchorage with him," Lacy interrupted. "With Raphael. I'm not …" She paused so she wouldn't fumble over her words. "I'm not choosing Raphael over you. It's been four years. Do you know how weird that is? He's been going to my dad's church. He's all religious now. Do you think I'm just going to throw away this life to be with someone I hardly know anymore?"

"Then why Anchorage? Why so fast?"

"I need to get out of here. I need time to think. Decide if I even want to keep living as Jo anymore." Her voice caught.

"And I can't make a decision like that while you're here being so nice and caring and understanding, and I can't do it with him spouting off Bible verses and talking about how it's some big miracle we found each other."

Kurtis frowned. "But don't you find it just a tad suspicious that after four years you just randomly bump into him, in Glennallen of all places?"

Lacy sat up in her seat. "I told you I'm not leaving with him. I need time to think, and I can't do that if both of you are …"

Her phone beeped. Probably another text from Raphael. She ignored it.

"I can't do that if both of you are trying to pressure me."

Kurtis relaxed in his chair. "So you're going to Anchorage to take a little time to figure things out. Is that it?"

"That's what I've been trying to tell you."

"And where does that leave me? What about this Raphael guy?"

"I already said I don't know. I can't be expected to make any decisions like this until I know more what I want. At this point, I'm thinking of just flying back to Boston and living my old life again."

"You can't do that. It wouldn't be safe."

"That's what you're telling me. But how am I supposed to know until I get a little breathing room and figure things out for myself?"

He sighed. "All right. I'm not going to try to stop you."

She eyed him quizzically. "You angry?"

He shook his head but remained quiet.

"You understand why I couldn't tell you the truth?"

"Of course. I'm a trooper, remember?"

She stood up. "You'll say good-bye to Madeline for me, right?"

"If that's what you want." He sighed. "Do you need a ride to town, or is he taking you?"

"I'm driving myself."

He raised an eyebrow. "Is your check oil light still blinking?"

"Only sometimes," she lied. She had forgotten all about that.

"Why don't you let me at least change it before you go?"

She stared at the door. "I'm sure I'll make it just fine."

"It's a four-hour trip, Jo."

"I know. I'll be ok."

Why couldn't he understand? Didn't he realize she couldn't keep accepting his help whenever a problem came up? Didn't

Alana Terry

he realize this move was something she had to do on her own?

She took a few steps toward the entryway but stopped and turned around. "I'm sorry. About everything."

He avoided her eyes. "Me, too."

She couldn't leave him like this. She inhaled deeply. "If I was Jo, you know I would have said yes yesterday and meant it."

"Yeah, I know."

He didn't stand up to see her out. As she passed the stairs to the basement, she heard the soundtrack to Madeline's princess movie playing softly. She paused for just a moment to listen and then opened the door and let herself out.

CHAPTER 8

The walk back to her apartment seemed to take hours. Was she really doing the right thing? Was she ready to pack and go? She felt bad leaving the daycare on short-notice, but Kim and one other part-time worker could pull together to make up her extra hours. Attendance was low this time of year anyway, with so many families going fishing or camping or vacationing in the Lower 48. She was probably doing the daycare's budget a big favor.

She thought about Carl and Sandy, about how easy it would be to hop on a plane and fly back to Massachusetts. If she had the money, that is. She could sell her car in town, maybe get one or two grand for it. That was a start. Enough to get her back home. Or put down a payment on an apartment in Anchorage. A very small apartment. What should she do?

"For I know the plans I have for you," declares the Lord. Yeah, well, so far his plans for her life hadn't worked out all that swimmingly. It was time for her to make her own

decisions. Make her own plans.

Whatever that meant.

She got home and pulled the small suitcase out from under her bed. Drisklay had told her to keep a small bag packed and ready so she could take off at a moment's notice if her cover was ever blown. She had packed it four years ago and never opened it since. She couldn't remember what was in it anymore. She took the contents out one at a time and laid them on her mattress. Two blouses. A pair of jeans. Hair brush, tooth brush, tooth paste. Socks, underclothes, and a coat. That was all. You could study the whole thing without learning anything about her except her bra size. How was it that her whole life had been stripped away from her until all that was left was this little carry-on full of belongings that meant nothing to her? It was because they weren't hers. They weren't Lacy's. They belonged to an imaginary woman named Jo who worked at a daycare, had never gone to college, and lived in a remote town in Alaska where the temperatures could drop to negative fifty over Thanksgiving.

She had been living Jo's life for too long.

She put the nondescript items back in the bag and pulled out a few more things from her closet. If she was staying in Alaska, she should take the heavy winter stuff she had accumulated. But if she went back to the East Coast …

No, she couldn't think like that. She hadn't made a single decision herself in four years, at least not an important one. Even dating Kurtis had felt like part of her cover story, not something she would have done if she were still living her own life, if she were still Lacy. She tried to ignore the memory of his expression when she left his house earlier. She had expected him to be hurt. Of course he would be. It would have been easier if he had tried to talk her out of moving or even lost his temper. Instead, he was so stoic, which wounded her even more deeply.

She sniffed, reminding herself that nothing was finalized. She might spend two days in Anchorage. She might spend two years. All that mattered was that this was a decision she was making for herself. Nobody was making it for her, no Boston detective, no larger-than-life boyfriend, no former love who had materialized out of nowhere after four years of torturous waiting.

Where she went after Anchorage was her choice as well. If she came back to Glennallen, that would be her decision and no one else's. Same thing if she returned to Massachusetts to be with Carl and Sandy. If she accepted Kurtis's proposal, or if she and Raphael resumed their romance after a four-year hiatus, or if she found someone else entirely down the road or chose to stay single for the rest of her life, those were decisions only she could make. She wouldn't let anybody dictate her life anymore.

Her phone beeped, and she realized she had missed several texts from Raphael. She was avoiding him. It was all so strange, his coming back from the dead. And all his talk now about God and the Bible and Carl's church? His family had been Catholic, if she remembered right. He came to church with her on holidays or if Carl and Sandy invited him over for lunch after the service, but it wasn't a big part of his life. Hers, either. They were too busy living to really settle down and dwell on the metaphysical for long. She knew there was a God, she knew the Bible was basically true, and she figured that one day she might actually study it on her own instead of just at the dining room table with her foster mom. How many Bible verses had Raphael mentioned last night when he came over? What had gotten a hold of him? She needed time to absorb it all. She sent him a text back. She had already decided she'd meet him for lunch and explain to him what she had just told Kurtis. She was going to Anchorage until she figured out her next move, and if Raphael was the same man he'd been four years ago, he'd be ok with that.

Her packing was interrupted by a knock on the door.

Kurtis? In all honesty, she would have felt hurt if he let her leave without trying to change her mind, but she wasn't ready. Not yet. She bustled into the kitchen, where a pile of dirty dishes overflowed from the sink onto the counter and stacked themselves into precarious three-dimensional shapes. Great. Her landlord would love her for this.

The knocking again. It wasn't like Kurtis to be impatient. Raphael, maybe? But she had just texted him and made plans to meet in an hour.

The door burst open. She slammed her rag onto the counter and stormed into the dining room. "What are you …"

She froze when she saw who it was.

"You didn't lock yourself in." Detective Drisklay stood in the middle of her living room, frowning. He pointed his paper coffee cup at her door. "How many times did we tell you to lock yourself in?"

Lacy couldn't move. Couldn't speak. Couldn't explain to him that this was Glennallen, Alaska, where people went on month-long vacations without locking up. While they were thawing out in Hawaii or whatever warm coast they escaped to, their neighbors brought in the mail and placed it on their dining room tables.

Drisklay pulled out the chair where Kurtis and Raphael had

both sat the night before. He was a detestable sight. Lacy didn't trust him enough to take her eyes off him. "What are you doing here?" she asked.

"You need to get your things together." He spoke so casually, as if they were discussing a piece of math homework.

Lacy had always despised math.

"You said we were done meeting face to face."

He shrugged and took a big swig of coffee. "Things change." Drisklay scanned her apartment. She knew he was taking everything in. He wouldn't miss a single detail. "So, how much time do you need to pack?"

The room was spinning. Her head was as light as the helium balloons Raphael had won for her at the Salem fair so many years ago. She steadied herself on the table. "Do I have to?"

He shrugged. "You're a free citizen, but obviously I can't guarantee your safety if you fail to comply."

"Why?" she demanded, ignoring the nagging suspicion growing in her gut.

"Your cover's blown. Someone in the trooper's office's getting a little too nosy."

"That was just Kurtis. He wouldn't …"

"We've never lost a placement yet," Drisklay interrupted.

"You think I want the first time to be on my watch?"

"Where do you want me to go?"

"You know the drill. You'll get all the details once you're safe. It's a total reboot. New papers, new name, the works. I'll use the bathroom while you get your bag. I assume you've kept one packed and ready like I told you."

Lacy forced herself to look at him in the eye even though her insides were quivering like one of the many minor tremors she had experienced since moving here. "No."

"No, you don't have a bag, or no you don't want me using the toilet? It's a long drive to Anchorage, you know."

She took a deep breath. "No, I'm not going with you. I'm not going through it all again."

He set his cup on the table and looked at her as if she had just told him she wanted to visit the moon because she was in the mood for some cheese. "So I guess you'll just sit tight here, wait for the Mafia to come into your unlocked house and finish what they set out to do four years ago?"

"The trial's over. Nobody has any reason to hurt me."

He frowned. "Revenge can be quite a strong motivation. Sometimes I think you fail to appreciate just how powerful these men are."

"I'm leaving Glennallen anyway. I don't need you to

relocate me."

He shrugged. "It's a free country, but I beg you to remember that these men know your identity."

Good, she thought to herself, *that means I can go back to being Lacy since the Jo cover's already blown.* "All you know for sure is that the trooper knows who I am, right? Good, because I just told him today when I broke off our engagement." She didn't know why she mentioned that part. What would Drisklay care?

He shrugged. "You think about it while I use your toilet."

After Lacy moved in with the Lindgrens, her foster mother told her, "Hatred is a force as strong as death itself." If that was true, Drisklay would have suffered a fatal catastrophe as he sauntered uninvited down her hall. Lacy stared at his half-empty coffee cup and wanted to spit in it. It was a childish gesture that wouldn't have solved anything except relieve her tension for a few seconds.

She ignored the sweaty, clammy feeling around the collar of her blouse. She had already resolved to get out of Glennallen, but there was no way she was going through an entire relocation with Drisklay and his cronies. She'd drive into Anchorage, slip in anonymously amongst the hundreds of thousands of people there, and stay put until she made up her mind. This was her life, her future, after all. Not his.

He came out of the bathroom and picked up his paper cup. "You ready? Where's your bag?"

"I said I'm not going."

"You were serious?" There was something in his dead-pan expression that might have been humorous under different circumstances.

She nodded.

He sighed. "I'll stick around through the end of the day. Call me when you come to your senses."

CHAPTER 9

Her whole body was shaking by the time Drisklay left, but she ignored the trembling and went back to her room to finish packing. Nothing could change her mind. Not now. She had regained control of her life for the first time since it started spinning rampant four years ago. She flipped through her wallet to see how much cash she had. Just enough to fill her tank and maybe buy a few groceries to start off in Anchorage. She didn't know anyone out there, but that didn't matter. Lacy was never afraid of meeting new people, seeing new places. This would be an adventure, an adventure she could determine for once.

Carl and Sandy would worry about her if they knew. They were always so safety conscious, which was probably why they were never thrilled with Raphael in the first place. But she didn't answer to them anymore, even though she hadn't stopped thinking of them since Raphael told her he went to their church. And if he was right, if Massachusetts was safe for her now, she could go home.

At last.

Of course, that was getting ahead of herself. First Anchorage. Give herself a few days to settle in. Decide from there what to do. It was too early to meet Raphael for lunch, but she was anxious to get on the road. There was nothing left for her here. Nothing but old memories, old identities.

And Kurtis.

Of course, there was still Kurtis.

But she'd have time to think about that in Anchorage. Her co-worker Kim had a sister in town. Maybe she needed a roommate. It was summer. Wouldn't there be a plethora of kids in need of nannies? Or she could go to the University of Alaska, fill out their application for student aid, get a dorm on campus. There were enough options she didn't need to worry. Everything was going to work itself out.

Finally.

She grabbed her suitcase and a backpack and threw them in her trunk, and then she came back to fill a Costco box with a few random items. The rest could go to whatever tenant took over after her. She wouldn't get her security deposit back after leaving the apartment such a mess, but once she sold her car, she wouldn't need the extra cash.

She took a deep breath.

Everything was going to be just fine.

She left her apartment keys on the dining room table, started up her car, and drove to the Elk Hotel. That was one nice thing about a town as small as Glennallen. There was only one place that lodged out-of-town guests. She hurried in and stopped at the front desk. "Hi, I have a friend staying here. I was wondering if you could call his room for me."

"What's his name?"

Lacy stopped. She didn't even know what alias Raphael was using. "Umm, can you try ..."

"Well, look who showed up!" His voice boomed from the top-level balcony as he leaned over with a grin. "I was just getting ready to text you. Give me a sec, and I'll be right down."

Lacy smiled sheepishly and waited near the stairs. She felt as anxious as she had at her junior prom. She kept fidgeting with her hands, wondering what he would do when he came down. She didn't feel ready for another kiss, even though that one last night had felt so good, if not long overdue.

Raphael was all smiles as he hustled down the stairs to his own syncopated rhythm. "How's my girl?" He placed his hand on the small of her back and noisily pecked the air about an inch away from her cheek in classic New England style. He still wore the same cologne, that inviting masculine scent. How had she lived the past four years without him? "What have you been up to? I thought you weren't free until later."

"Plans changed. I, um …" She glanced at the desk clerk. "Well, you want to head outside? Go on a walk or something?"

His eyes darted to the window. "Sure. My bike's locked up and secure. I'm all yours."

They stepped outside, and Lacy swatted away the mosquitoes that swarmed her face. She took her hair out of her ponytail to give her ears and neck more protection. "I've been thinking," she began tentatively, "and I've got to tell you some things. Part of it's good, and part of it's not." There, was that enough of a warning?

He walked beside her with his familiar, easy step. She had forgotten the simple joy of being beside him, being together, enjoying the outdoors. The Wrangell Mountains stretched out before them, tiny dollops of snow from last winter still capping the peaks. He slipped his arm around her waist, unassuming. Natural. "Start with the good stuff."

"Well, I've made up my mind about a few things. I went over to see …" She faltered before saying his name. It sounded so strange talking about him. "I went to see my trooper friend. And, well, I said I was going to Anchorage to give myself time to put everything together."

Raphael nodded thoughtfully. "Sounds reasonable. He took it ok?"

"Yeah." She wasn't willing to get into details of their conversation and was glad he didn't press it any further.

"What's the bad news, then?"

She slowed her pace. "Well, I feel like in some ways I need to have the same conversation with you. I mean, I'm thrilled you're here, but before I go anywhere, before I make any big decisions about our relationship, I need time to think through it all."

He let out a little laugh. "You have no idea how glad I am to hear you say that."

"Really?"

"Well, it's weird for me too, you know. I mean, don't get me wrong. I was so excited last night I only slept for two hours, but on the other hand, it's like we've been living totally separate lives these past four years. We're different people, whether we want to admit it or not. And well, as stoked as I am to imagine what God might have in store for us, I think it's good to slow down a little. Give ourselves time to think things through. Pray about it. Make sure we're doing the right things for the right reasons, you know?"

She nodded, taken slightly aback. She had expected this conversation to be harder.

"So Anchorage, huh?" he said after a minute. "What will you be doing once you're there?"

"I don't even know what I want to do anymore."

"You ever think of going back to school?"

"Maybe, but I'd have to start over at the beginning. All of my credits are under my old name ..." Her voice trailed off, and neither of them said anything. She wondered if he was thinking the same thing she was. She could go back to Lacy. There was always that option. Transfer her old credits to UAA, enroll in ...

No, she was moving to Anchorage so she had time to think. She couldn't get ahead of herself.

They reached the end of the sidewalk and turned around automatically. Raphael glanced at the time on his phone. "It's a little past eleven. Is that too early for lunch?"

"Actually, I'm leaving today. I guess that's the rest of the bad news." Had she told him that part yet? "It's not because of you or anything, I just ..."

"I know. You're itching to be alone and make sense of everything. And when I'm around that just confuses the matter."

"That's not what I ..."

"I'm just teasing." He nudged her playfully. "Well, I got to get to Anchorage, too. Care to drive with me?"

"Nah, I'm taking my car. I'm selling it for my seed money."

"Not a bad idea." He sighed. "Does that mean no lunch?"

She could hear the disappointment in his tone. "Well, what if we make a date in Anchorage?" she asked. "Dinner tonight?"

A grin spread across his face. "Deal. I'm buying."

She grinned, too. "Good, because I'm officially broke."

"Hey, do you want me to …" He stopped on the sidewalk and fidgeted in his pocket. "We could find an ATM and I could let you have …"

She shook her head. "No. This move, getting away from here, everything, I've got to do this on my own." How could she explain it to him? How could she explain how she could never really find out if she was Jo or Lacy or some other stranger she hadn't even met yet until she went through this alone? "But thanks." She let her hand rest on his shoulder for a moment. Their eyes locked.

He gave her a smile. "You got this, Lace."

Deep in her heart, she knew he was right.

CHAPTER 10

She said good-bye to Raphael when they reached the hotel again. It was easier knowing she would see him in Anchorage at the end of the day. Maybe the drive would give her time to think through things a little more. Maybe by dinner, she'd have formed some kind of plan for the next few weeks. Tonight they would meet in Anchorage as free adults. The thought made her almost giddy as she crossed the street to Puck's grocery store. She had about a hundred dollars left in her bank account. In a week, she'd get her last paycheck from the daycare. Money might be tight in Anchorage, but it wasn't as though she had made it big wiping snotty noses on the playground, either.

She was on the road fifteen minutes later, speeding out of Glennallen, heading for a new life. Her enthusiasm was short-lived, however. She had just passed the native church in Mendeltna when her change oil light flickered. Her car sputtered and lost speed. She pushed down again on the accelerator, but the engine ground in protest.

Flipping on her emergency lights, she eased over onto the side of the road. Thankfully, nobody was behind her. She tried to pick up speed, but the engine shuddered once more and then died. So much for that idea. For the faintest moment, she wondered if Drisklay had sabotaged her car. He was so convinced she needed to stay in the program. Maybe he got kickbacks based on how many protectees he kept corralled in their rightful places.

She flipped on her cell phone. Coverage was spotty from here most of the way to Anchorage. She got a faint signal and spent another two or three minutes deciding who to call. She gave one final attempt to turn the engine over. It coughed faintly before grinding again.

Nothing.

She had to go back. For a minute, she thought about walking all the way to Glennallen, but that was ridiculous. It would take her half the day, and the bugs were atrocious. She needed to call for a ride.

Call who? Kurtis? Raphael?

She looked at both men's names in her cell phone, testing each one out in her mind. Kurtis would drop everything, bring Madeline with him, and probably find a way to tow her car back to Glennallen. He'd spend the rest of his day off fixing it in his garage. Could she expect him to do that after the way she'd treated him?

She could ask Raphael to pick her up. It would give them more time to talk, but the most he could do would be to drive her back to Glennallen, where she'd probably end up needing Kurtis to help get her car anyway.

She sighed. Was this fate? God's way of keeping her humble right when she thought she was figuring out how to live once more? She thought again of Drisklay and pictured how smug he would look if he saw her here stranded on the side of the road.

She had hesitated long enough. She pulled Kurtis's number up on her cell phone and bit her lip, fighting to keep from hanging up before he answered.

"Hello?"

"It's me. I hate to do this to you, but I had some car trouble outside of Mendeltna. Can you come get me?"

Silence. What was he thinking?

"The oil?"

"Yeah." Why hadn't she listened to him? He had been harping about that change oil light since spring.

A sigh. "All right. The munchkin's in the bath right now. It'll be a few minutes."

"Take your time. I'm not going anywhere." A week ago, they probably would have both laughed.

More silence. For a minute, she wondered if he would ask her why she hadn't called Raphael.

"I'm sorry," she added.

"It's not a problem. Give me half an hour to dry her off and get to you."

"Thanks," she added, but he had already hung up.

CHAPTER 11

Getting stranded on a stretch of the Glenn Highway as scenic as Mendeltna might not have been quite so terrible if she had thought to bring bug spray with her. She locked herself in the car and killed three mosquitoes before the buzzing finally stopped. At least it wasn't too hot. Half an hour. It wasn't a big deal. It's not like she had anywhere to rush to in Anchorage. She didn't even know where she'd be spending the night. She should take advantage of the time to finish off some business. Like telling the daycare she was leaving. And asking Kim if her sister knew of anybody in town who needed a nanny or house-sitter or roommate. But she was too mentally exhausted. She thought about her conversation with Raphael, how he said he had hardly slept more than a few hours last night. He was so excited. Sometimes she wondered why she wasn't more so. Was it the religion thing? Raphael had always been a decent person, but it was strange to hear all those churchy things coming out of his mouth. He sounded like her foster dad.

She had been thinking of Carl and Sandy more and more since Raphael showed up. She wouldn't be surprised if that was where her future would eventually take her. She had never really considered Anchorage the final destination, more like a time-out of sorts, a chance to rest and revive and take inventory on what she wanted out of life.

What she really wanted was her identity back, but even if that was safe, she wasn't sure how it would work. Would she just go to Drisklay and demand her old birth certificate and photo ID? What kind of paperwork would be involved in something like that? Would it be as formal as when she joined the witness protection program and became Jo in the first place? What if Drisklay wouldn't cooperate? What if he was so offended she didn't stick it out in his program that he refused to give her the right papers back, refused to let her resume her old identity?

As long as she was living the life she wanted, did it really matter? Why couldn't she do what Raphael had done, go back home but keep living under her new name? Well, she would have time to figure all that out in Anchorage. Right now, she just needed to wait, needed to sit tight until Kurtis got here.

Why did it have to be him? Maybe because he was the only person she knew very well in Glennallen, her only real friend. If he was even that anymore. There was so much she had to think about, so much to mull over.

A car pulled up behind her, and she turned the emergency lights off. That was one nice thing about this part of the country. Roadside assistance didn't come from insurance companies. It came from good Samaritans. She rolled down her window to wave the stranger past but stopped when she saw who it was.

"What are you doing here?" She stepped out of the car.

Raphael was smiling his mischievous grin. "What are *you* doing here?"

"Car trouble," she admitted.

"Can I help?"

"Not unless you've gotten handier with mechanics than you were four years ago."

They both chuckled. It felt good to laugh.

"But really," she said, "what are you doing here?"

He shrugged. "I figured I'd hit the road. There wasn't much to do in Glennallen but sit around and watch the maids clean the rooms. I left not long after you did. Good thing, too, I guess." He glanced at her car. "Do you know what's wrong?"

"I have someone coming over to take a look." She didn't want to admit the whole thing had been her fault. Why hadn't she let Kurtis take a look at the oil when he offered?

Raphael just nodded. She was glad he didn't pry.

"Want to hop in?" he asked. "We're going the same way."

She didn't turn him down automatically. She needed her car for the money, but then again, how could she sell a vehicle that didn't work? She still felt bad about pulling Kurtis away from his day off, too, and would be happy to tell him he didn't have to come out after all. More than anything, she would be glad for an excuse to not see him again, at least not right away.

"You know what," she said, surprising herself by how readily she made up her mind, "I think I'll do that, if you're sure it's ok with you."

He gave a half-grin. "Just don't spill your Coke on my seat like you did driving to that show in Baltimore. You remember that?"

She laughed and popped open her trunk. "That's not fair. I would have never spilled it if you hadn't sped around that corner."

"How was I supposed to know there were speed bumps all up and down that road?" he asked, grabbing her two bags.

"I don't know," she countered playfully. "Maybe you could have read one of the *signs* on the road, or is that too easy of an answer?" She took the Costco box and carried it to his backseat. "Is there room for all this?"

He took down his bike from its rack and hefted her things into his trunk. "Oh, yeah. You know me, still traveling light after all these years, except now I travel with the Holy Spirit."

Her smile dropped. Her neck and shoulders ached with heaviness.

"What's wrong?" he asked.

"Two minutes. We almost made it two whole minutes before you started talking church."

He hooked his bike back onto the rack. "Does it offend you?"

She shook her head. "No, it's not that. It's just, I feel like I hardly know you anymore. You sound like my dad when he preaches, and I just …"

He tucked a strand of her hair behind her ear. "Hey, it's cool. I don't want to shove anything down your throat. But you know me. When I get a good thing going for me, I get excited."

"I know. And I didn't mean to sound critical, it's just …" She didn't know how to finish.

"A lot has happened these past four years. It's gonna take us some time."

"Yeah."

They both got into their seats.

"So, what are you gonna do about your car?" he asked.

She wished she could just leave it there and let someone else deal with it. "I guess I'll see if my friend can tow it back to Glennallen for me."

"You can say his name, you know."

Lacy avoided his eyes.

"The trooper you were seeing. He has a name, I assume."

"Yeah." She bit her lip. "Hey, do you mind if I hop out and make a phone call real quick? I'll be right back."

"Sure." He still had that same jocular smile. He glanced around once. "Just don't take too long. These bugs are terrible."

CHAPTER 12

A minute later, Lacy was back in Raphael's car, on the highway speeding toward Anchorage. She hadn't been able to get hold of Kurtis, but she left a message to tell him she had a ride and to ask him if he'd mind towing the car to Glennallen until she figured out what to do with it. She offered to pay him for his time once she got settled in, even though she knew he'd never take her money. She still wasn't sure she had made the right decision, but if the car was busted, it could be days or weeks before she got out of Glennallen. By then, she might lose her fortitude. She had to do this now. It was the only way.

She tried not to think about Kurtis. She should have never asked him for help with the car in the first place. Oh well, it was too late now. He was probably already on the road, already in a no-coverage zone. Should she have left him a note on her dashboard to explain what was happening?

The longer they drove, the more she realized she wouldn't be coming back to Glennallen. She was tired of the daycare, sick of the bratty attitudes, the whiny voices, the kids complaining when they had no idea how good their lives really were. She was tired of everything, really, tired of the long winters, the bug-infested summers. There was no fall to speak of here, and spring just meant everything was gray and mushy while the piles of snow melted.

"You tired?" Raphael asked, stealing a quick glance at her.

"Yeah." She was surprised again at how uncomfortable it was with him. Ironic, really, that she had dreamed for so long of meeting him again, and now that they were in the same car, she could hardly put two words together.

Raphael put on his sunglasses. "I've got some snacks in the back. You hungry?"

"No. Thanks."

"So, you got everything you'll need? Passport, all that stuff from witness protection?"

She nodded, tired of the awkward chitchat, and stared at the scenery. Even in summer, the evergreens along this stretch the highway looked dried out and dead, more brown on top than green. Why did everyone always talk about how beautiful Alaska was? Was there anything she would miss about life out here?

There was Kurtis, of course, but he had never really known

her. Sure, he put enough details together to figure out her true identity, but that didn't mean he knew her. He didn't know her favorite Boston restaurants, the kind of paintings she was drawn to, which conductors of which East Coast symphonies she liked best. He didn't know she was on first-name basis with a handful of art critics, or that she had once studied theater under a Tony Award nominee.

She thought she would be relieved to leave Glennallen. Where was the sense of freedom she had expected?

Change is always hard, she reminded herself, but at least this was one change she could control, not like her placement in Glennallen four years ago. So why did she feel like a little girl again getting driven from one foster home to another?

"I hope your car's all right." Raphael and she had never struggled in the past to find things to talk about. What was the problem?

He took a deep breath as if he was about to speak but remained silent. She grabbed her purse and fumbled through the contents, unsure what in particular she was searching for.

"What do you need?" he asked.

"Just looking for my Dramamine."

He smiled. "You and your motion sickness. I guess some things don't change, do they?"

"Not on these windy roads," she murmured, and remembered she had used the last pill on her most recent trip to town with Kurtis.

Raphael ducked down and craned his neck. "Whoa, look at that! Is that a bald eagle?" He pointed at a shadow out his window.

Lacy couldn't remember how many eagles she had spotted before she stopped seeing them as beautiful, majestic creatures and started viewing them as the disgusting rot-eaters they really were.

"Careful." She resisted the urge to reach over and steer for him.

"I'm paying attention." He put both hands back on the wheel.

"Sorry. It's just this part of the highway makes me nervous." They were speeding along the edge of a mountain, a single lane away from a five-hundred-foot cliff.

"I'll be careful," Raphael promised.

"You might want to slow down a little." She eyed his speedometer. He wasn't used to this kind of driving. The East Coast didn't have mountain stretches like this. Not with such terrifying drop-offs.

They also believed in something called guard rails.

"As you wish." The familiar hint of mischief was back in his voice, and Lacy realized he hadn't spoken about his new zeal for the Bible or Christianity since they got on the road. Had she offended him in Mendeltna?

"So," he went on, "have you thought about calling Carl and Sandy? I know they'd love to hear from you."

There was so much she wanted to tell him, about her conversation with Drisklay, about how Kurtis had gotten in touch with her foster parents. "That would be nice," was all she replied. She stared out the window and wondered for the second time if she should ask him to turn around. How rude could she be, expecting Kurtis to tow her car all the way to Glennallen for her when she doubted she'd ever return? She had just dumped it in his lap on his day off, expecting him to drag Madeline out of the bath, get her dressed, drive twenty minutes, hook his truck up … Could she get any more selfish?

She pulled out her phone. "Hey, would it be weird for you if I called just to check in about the car? I feel pretty bad just dropping it on him like that."

"Of course not."

Lacy turned on her phone and then flipped it back off. Stupid cell phone reception.

"Not there?" Raphael asked.

95

"Bad coverage." Stupid state.

"Want to turn around? Meet him back there?"

The last thing Lacy needed was to be around both Raphael and Kurtis at once. Her life was confusing enough already. She wasn't technically dating either of them, but on the other hand, she hadn't broken up with them either. Of course, you can't break up with somebody who's been murdered. She'd been right about the detectives faking Raphael's death. A trick from the folks at witness protection so everyone would think he was murdered until he appeared at the trial. She had waited. Hoped …

"Why weren't you there?" she asked quietly.

"What?"

"At the trial," she explained. "I kept expecting them to call you to testify. I kept hoping you'd show up. But you never did."

"That's a good question." His voice was strained. A little more uncertain. Not like Raphael at all. He glanced over at her and sighed. "Listen, I need to make a confession. You're not gonna like it."

CHAPTER 13

"About that trial ..." Raphael's fingers tensed on the steering wheel. He scratched the back of his neck. "This isn't easy to talk about, you know. But I guess you deserve an explanation. So, the short version ... wait, is that my phone beeping or yours?"

Lacy opened her purse. She had missed two calls from Kurtis and one from a blocked number. "Hold on," she said, unsure if she was ready for whatever Raphael was going to say. "Let me see if I can get any coverage here."

She called Kurtis back, but it went right to his voicemail. Fine with her. She was already experiencing about as much awkwardness as one person could handle. "What were you saying?"

Raphael adjusted his sunglasses. "So anyway, about the trial. I think for everything to make sense, we need to rewind. Go all the way back to the accident."

Lacy's whole body tensed. She didn't realize she was

gripping her seatbelt until her fingers started to hurt.

"There's a lot about that night you don't know. And it's been eating me up since it happened. And, well, it's not gonna be easy for you to hear."

The car was rushing. Too fast. She checked the speedometer. Only fifty? It felt like twice that.

"So those men on the dock, everything that happened …" He swallowed once and reached for her hand which fell limp in his. "It wasn't an accident. Not really. And I've never forgiven myself for it because it was my fault. In a way."

She wanted him to turn around. Wanted to go home.

"I'd gotten myself into a mess." The words tumbled out of his mouth. She couldn't stop them. Like a deadly avalanche. "You know me. You know how I was back then. I wasn't the smartest kid, made some dumb choices, but I never got into the really bad stuff."

Lacy felt just like she did on rollercoasters. Everything whizzed by, gaining momentum. There was no way to get off once you were strapped in. The exit came after the ride was over, after your stomach was lodged up in the top of your chest and your throat was sore from screaming and your fingers were numb from gripping your restraint. The only difference was this particular ride wasn't fun or exciting or adventurous. And there was no way to gauge how long it would last before it ended.

"I had some guys mad at me. I was out of my league. Way out of my league. You know I wasn't the type to go digging for trouble. I just wanted to live simply. Me, you, my art. I would have been happy with just that. I should have been happy with that. But, well, things happened. I made some bad choices, got mixed up with the wrong people."

Lacy didn't care. She wanted him to stop talking. Erase time. Make it so the past four years never happened. People always talked about how struggles make you wiser. More mature. Not the accident. It had robbed her. Stolen her identity, torn her from her boyfriend, and botched her entire future.

Her entire future.

Where would she be now if it hadn't been for that night in the North End? She'd have finished her bachelor's degree. She and Raphael would have gotten married, wouldn't they? Of course, they would. How many art galas had she missed in the past four years? How many concerts? How many Broadway shows? Would she have continued to pursue her acting career? Would anything have come of it?

She'd never know. The accident stripped all that away from her. She had blamed God. Blamed the car. Blamed Drisklay. Blamed the criminals who waltzed into her field of vision to dump a living person into the wharf. In all this time, she had always thought of Raphael as a victim as well.

Had she been mistaken?

"I was going to propose to you that night."

It was the last thing she wanted to hear. She gripped the handle of the car door, her mind begging for an escape.

"I had the ring in my coat pocket and everything," he continued. "But I was in this mess I told you about. I had to get away. Lie low for a while. I was gonna tell you all this that night at the pier. I swear …" His voice caught, and Lacy wanted to clear her throat on his behalf. "I spent so many nights awake, wondering what to do. I couldn't sleep. Couldn't eat. Couldn't paint. I knew I had to skip town. I couldn't stand the thought of leaving you, but how could I ask you to go with me? Leave your foster family, your classes, everything you'd known."

Her throat muscles clenched. She would have given up all her plans to be with him, would have given them up in an instant. Instead, every single dream was shattered like broken glass, and she went four years without even knowing if he was alive.

"I took you to the pier to tell you everything. Come clean. Geeze, Lace, you have no idea how messed up I was. I had this show I was supposed to be getting ready for, the one at the

Menagerie …"

"I remember," she whispered as flooding memories came crashing over her. Suffocating her.

"And I hadn't been able to paint in two weeks. I was so torn. Finally, I realized all I could do was come clean. Tell you everything. And then, if you'd still have me, I was gonna ask you to leave with me. I had a plan. There was a guy. He was gonna meet me at the pier. He was gonna help us get …"

"Is that who they killed?" she whispered.

Raphael's throat worked loudly. "I never meant to get you involved in any of this." He squeaked out the last words. "I'm so sorry."

He sniffed. She couldn't look at him. Couldn't handle the torrent of emotions that would drown her if she saw his tears.

"You hate me, don't you?" he asked.

She took in a choppy breath. "I don't know what you did to make those guys so mad at you." She thought back over her relationship with Raphael. The romance. Passion. Adventures. Friendship. "All I know is I was in love with you. I would have gone with you anywhere." She swallowed away a painful lump.

"Anywhere," she repeated, the word searing hot in her throat.

CHAPTER 14

Lacy's phone rang, freeing her from the weight of Raphael's confession. She hesitated and then held up her finger to Raphael before answering. "Hello?"

"Jo? It's me. Where are you?"

Raphael shot her a nervous glance. Was he worried she would change her mind? Why shouldn't she after what he had just told her?

"We just passed Eureka. Did you find where I left the car?"

"Yeah, and …"

She strained her ears. "You're breaking up. Can you say that again?"

More static.

"Hello?" She waited another few seconds and then hung up. Stupid cell reception.

"Everything ok?" Raphael asked.

"Yeah, just a bad signal." She was so sick of this state, so sick of its backwards technology, its ridiculous bugs. A mosquito the size of a New England housefly landed on her. She slapped it, splattering blood all over herself. "Gross." She flipped open the glove compartment. "Do you have any napkins or anything?"

The compartment was empty except for a piece of paper from a car rental place with a strange name filled out at the top.

Maxwell Turner? It didn't sound like Raphael at all. Another imperfect fit. Just like Jo.

She glanced at the form again and saw yesterday's date stamped in the top corner.

Yesterday's? Didn't he say he'd been in Alaska for weeks?

"No, I don't have anything in there." Raphael reached to shut the glove compartment.

"Rats." She forced a laugh. "I hate it when I squash a bloody one."

Snippets from her conversation with Drisklay ran through her mind. *Cover's blown. Someone getting a little too nosy ...* Raphael himself had just admitted to having connections with the murderers on the pier.

"I'm not feeling good." She tried to make her voice sound natural.

"Need to roll your window down?"

"No, I really think I'm about to be sick. Can you pull

over?"

"Sure. Let me just get us to a shoulder."

She grabbed the door handle. "No, pull over now. I'm gonna throw up." At the rate things were going, she wouldn't need to pretend.

"Ok." He eased to the side of the road. Think. She had to think.

Her cover was blown. Drisklay had flown out here to tell her that. She thought it was Kurtis putting pieces together, calling her foster parents. But what if it was something else? What if she was wrong?

Why would Raphael make up a story about being in Alaska for weeks if he just got here yesterday? He had already acknowledged his connection to the North End criminals. Could he be part of ...

No, this was Raphael. They had spent two and a half years almost inseparable before the accident. They knew everything about each other.

Everything.

He had found her so easily at the Brain Freeze. Like he had known right where to look ...

She was outside of the car, bent over. They couldn't stay here for long. The road wound so much that cars behind them wouldn't see them in time to stop. But what could she do? Flag down the next motorist? Take her chances and try to run?

A green car whizzed around a bend, speeding toward them from the opposite side of the road. It slowed down for a second as if the driver knew Lacy was in trouble.

"Oh, no."

Something about Raphael's tone sent goose bumps springing up on Lacy's neck.

"Get in the car." He reached across and tugged the back of her blouse. "Get in now." He checked his side mirror nervously. "Buckle up." He pulled her into the car and slammed on the gas before she could even shut the door.

"What are you doing?"

"We've got to go. Now." His voice was scared. Tense.

That's when she realized what a horrible mistake she had made. "I changed my mind," she blurted. "I want to go back."

"What?"

"Please. My whole life has been in Glennallen. I'm not ready to give all that up yet."

He took in a deep breath. "I don't think now's the best time for …"

"I was confused. Please. Just take me home." Her heart was racing. He was going to refuse. He wouldn't let her go. This had been …

"Listen." His voice was strained. His knuckles were white against the steering wheel. "I need you to stay calm and do exactly what I say."

Her phone beeped, and she pulled it out of her purse, relieved to finally be in an area with reception. She had to tell Kurtis what was happening. She glanced down at the screen. He had left her over a dozen texts over the past twenty-five minutes.

Car's tampered with. Get back here.
Pick up your phone. Where are you?
Get him to turn around.
Sit tight. We're on our way.

CHAPTER 15

"Please take me back." She heard the anxious edge in her own voice. She had to tone it down. Calm her nerves.

She angled the screen so Raphael couldn't read the texts. Could she really have misjudged him so drastically? The more she fought against the inevitable conclusion, the more sense it all made. Why he missed the trial. Why he was able to find her so easily in Glennallen. Why Drisklay had come to warn her.

She took in shallow breaths, afraid Raphael could hear how nervous she was. Good thing she had taken so many acting classes. Good thing she had spent four whole years living as another human being. If anyone could keep up a charade to survive, she could. She looked around. Was there anything she could use as a weapon? What if he tried to throw her out the car? On one side of them jutting straight up was the mountain, cruel and unyielding. On the other side a two-hundred-yard drop. She glanced at him without turning her head. Couldn't arouse his suspicion.

Kurtis, where are you?

"It could have been perfect between us, Lace," Raphael mused. She wasn't sure if she was supposed to play along or not. "It's like some gut-wrenching tragedy, where life just gets in the way."

"Please, I want to go home." What did she have in her purse? A cell phone. A wallet with her fake ID. What could she do, shove it down his throat?

"You have no idea how much I loved you."

Either he was just a good an actor as she, or he was planning something desperate. Her lungs worked in fractions. Labored jerks. So much for that deep diaphragm breathing her acting teachers always advocated.

"I just want you to turn around." Maybe she was wrong. Maybe Drisklay's visit had hurled her over the edge. Made her paranoid. Tonight she and Raphael would sit across from each other at an Anchorage restaurant and laugh.

Please, God?

Facts didn't lie. Dates didn't lie. She had to refocus her energy. Stop trying to deny the truth and find a way to get herself out of this mess alive.

"Turn around." She spoke each word succinctly. Strongly.

He glanced in the rear-view mirror. "Why?"

"Take me home, or I swear I'm calling the cops."

"What's going on, Lace?" he asked. The way he spoke her name made her stomach churn.

She couldn't do this. Couldn't pretend anymore. Couldn't pretend she was calm and collected. Couldn't pretend she wasn't scared. So scared she was either going to pee or throw up. Maybe both.

"The date's wrong." The accusation tumbled out of her mouth. "The one on your car rental papers. It says you got here yesterday."

Raphael let out his breath in a loud *huff*. "That's because I got tired and decided to drive to Anchorage instead of riding my bike back like I first planned. Geeze, Lace, is this an interrogation?"

She didn't speak.

He let out a sigh. "After everything we've been through together, the least you could do is trust me."

Could she?

Shame heated her cheeks. She stared at her lap.

He cleared his throat. Threw his glance in the rear-view mirror once more. "It happens to me, too. All the time. Like I think I see someone following me. Or I hear someone trying to break in at night." His chuckle was discordant. Unconvincing.

He patted her knee. "This whole ordeal turned me into a nervous wreck." He let out his breath.

Her hand still clenched the door handle.

"If you want the whole truth, I'm not up here just to cross Alaska off my bucket list. I was running away."

Her whole body was tense. The road twisted ahead of them and disappeared around the mountain bend.

"I went to a public art show at the Commons last month and thought I saw someone there. One of the men I'd gotten involved with before the accident."

She shut her eyes. Could you disappear by sheer force of will?

"A few days later, I thought someone was following me. So I headed out here until I could figure out what to do."

She didn't know if she believed him or not. All she knew was she wanted to go home.

"That green Dodge that we passed earlier," he went on. "I didn't get a good look, but for a second I thought it was the same guy." He let out a sad-sounding chuckle. "I told you, this whole way of living will make anybody paranoid."

A horn blared behind them. Lacy's eyes shot to her side mirror. It was the same Dodge they had seen. It must have turned around, because now it was directly behind them.

Speeding straight toward them.

Raphael swerved into the left lane. They were so close to the drop-off Lacy could feel the front wheel tilt before the car corrected itself.

The Dodge whizzed by and slammed on its brakes in the middle of the road. Raphael tried to pass on the right, but there wasn't enough room to clear the mountain. The passenger mirror flew off. The whole side of the car scraped against the rocks, the screeching sound grating in her ears even louder than her scream.

The Dodge pressed against them. Was it trying to squeeze them into the mountainside? Raphael slammed on his brakes. Lacy's body flew forward. The seatbelt jolted against her collarbone. "Who is that?" she demanded.

"It must be someone who knows about us."

"Us?"

"I'm sorry, Lace. I never wanted you to get caught up in any of this."

The Dodge had switched to reverse and was about to ram its bumper into them. "Move!" Lacy reached for the steering wheel, but Raphael had already jerked it to the side. The Dodge plowed into the back seat instead of straight on, but the momentum was almost enough to push them off the road.

111

Lacy's head was light, a helium balloon ready to float off into the clouds.

The Dodge pulled ahead.

"Hold on," Raphael told her. "He's coming at us again." The green car jerked to a stop, shooting a small pebble onto the windshield of the rental, creating a small chink in the glass. Lacy winced. Raphael had time to angle the car and pull up a few feet before the Dodge rammed them again in reverse.

"Are you ok?" Lacy could only take in the choppiest of breaths.

"I'm gonna turn us around." Raphael maneuvered the car on the narrow pass while the Dodge pulled ahead. Lacy gripped the door handle, holding her breath and praying he wouldn't misjudge and send them flying off the road. As soon as Raphael straightened his car, the Dodge flipped itself around in a three-point turn. The sound of her own pulse flooded Lacy's ears.

"Careful," she begged, her heart fluttering all the way up by her throat.

Raphael sped ahead. They were back on their way to Glennallen, but the Dodge was right behind them. And now they were driving on the other side of the road, the cliff's edge about a foot and a half away from Lacy's shoulder. She sucked in her breath, dizzy with fear, terrified that an extra ounce of weight might tilt the car off balance and send them careening to their deaths.

"I'm sorry," Raphael panted.

She didn't care. It didn't matter what he was apologizing for. It didn't matter what alias he used, or whether he rented his car yesterday or three weeks ago. All that mattered was they were speeding back in the direction of home. Toward Kurtis. Toward safety.

Her phone beeped. New voicemail. Did that mean there was coverage here? She pulled it out and dialed 911.

"Hold on!" Raphael shot his arm out across her chest right as the Dodge hit them from behind. Their car lurched forward to the sound of metal crumpling. Lacy's head whipped forward and then snapped back with so much force she couldn't see anything but black for a second. She wanted to ask Raphael what was happening, but she didn't have the breath to make herself heard.

"Can't this thing go any faster?" Raphael grumbled.

Her phone beeped again and flashed its ominous message. *Call failed.* Why had she ever moved to Alaska? She hated living here. She certainly didn't want to die here.

Raphael maneuvered around a hairpin curve without slowing down. She sucked in her breath, certain they were about to free-fall off the cliff. The speedometer raced past seventy. She clutched the door handle. *Let me out*, she wanted to beg, but she couldn't find her voice.

The car made it around the bend, and Lacy had a clear view of a straight stretch of road ahead with a red truck coming their way. "Is that ..." she started to ask but stopped, afraid to hold onto hope until she knew for sure. She waited for Raphael to get closer, begging God for deliverance. The Dodge had slowed down around the curve but was gaining momentum behind them.

The truck sped toward them. "That's Kurtis!" Lacy shouted. She recognized Drisklay in the passenger seat but didn't even wonder what he was doing there. It didn't matter. Kurtis was here. He would find a way to help. He was a trooper. He was trained. He'd know what to do.

Everything was going to be just ... Hope froze in Lacy's veins. What if Kurtis had Madeline in the truck with him? What if something happened to her?

Kurtis slowed down to let Raphael pass and gave what Lacy thought was a brief nod. She turned around to watch what would happen next. Kurtis's truck was in the middle of the road now. Was he trying to keep the Dodge from passing? What if he got hit? She scrunched down in her seat, trying to brace for the sound of the two vehicles crashing, praying Madeline was somewhere far away from all this.

The Dodge swerved, barely squeezing between Kurtis's truck and the rocky mountainside.

"Let me out. Let me get in with Kurtis."

"I can't do that," Raphael answered in a monotone.

No amount of Dramamine would cure this kind of sickness. Kurtis had turned his truck around and was coming up behind them.

"Let me out," she repeated.

"You have to trust me."

She stared over her shoulder. Was it possible the Dodge was falling back? Kurtis's truck came roaring up around the bend behind them. She squinted to avoid seeing the crash that never came.

"I know I've done some horrible things in my life," Raphael said. "But I'm telling the truth when I say I never wanted you to get messed up in all this. Just like I'm telling the truth when I say I've always …"

He sped around another curve, and Lacy gripped her seatbelt as the car wavered, struggling to keep its center of balance. She let out her breath when it straightened out, relieved for a short second.

"Look out!" Her warning was accompanied by a blaring horn from an RV camper directly in front of them. Raphael had swerved into the oncoming lane. There was no way they could avoid it. Lacy shot out her hands to brace for the impact.

But instead of crashing, they gained speed. She peeked at Raphael, who was frantically trying to gain control of the steering wheel. A shadow whizzed past her window. Tree branches scraped at the sides of the car.

They were rushing down the cliff.

She was deafened by the sound of her own scream. She grabbed the bottom of her seat and shut her eyes. Faster. A bump, and they were airborne. They landed again, and the bottom of the car scraped the rocky edge, but they hadn't reached the valley yet. They weren't slowing down, either. She opened her eyes. The view from the window turned and spiraled. They were spinning. She stopped screaming long enough to catch her breath and then began again. She had no idea how much longer they'd plunge until they hit the bottom, but she doubted she'd still be alive when they did.

CHAPTER 16

"It's ok. You're going to be just fine." She heard the voice but couldn't see anything. She tried to open her eyes. Only blackness. She blinked again. Nothing.

"I'm here." A hand reaching out to her. She was pinned down, trapped. The voice was soothing. "Can you move?"

I think I'm dead. She said the words but couldn't hear them.

"Drisklay's calling the ambulance. They'll get you to Anchorage. You're going to make it. Just hang in there."

She recognized that voice.

"Kurtis." This time her mouth managed to form the sounds.

"It's me." He squeezed her hand. "Save your energy. I'm right here. You're safe. I'm not leaving you."

She blinked again. Bright light from above pierced through the veil of darkness. She saw shadows but not distinct forms. Her head felt disconnected from the rest of her body.

"Where's the munchkin?" Her mouth was so dry she

couldn't form any more words.

"Shh." He patted her hand. Brushed some of her hair out of her eyes. "I dropped her off with another trooper's family. You remember Taylor, right? Don't talk. Just hang tight."

I'm gonna take a nap now. She only had enough energy to form the thought before she blacked out.

***

A horrific, grating noise, louder than any chainsaw.

Men yelling over the racket.

A presence by her side. Constant reassurance.

"She's going to be ok, isn't she?" Pleading in his voice.

She strained to hear the answer before everything fell once more to inky, black silence.

***

"You are one lucky girl."

Her eyes were so dry it took several attempts to blink them open. Drisklay sat next to her, sipping from a Styrofoam coffee cup.

She tried to speak, but her tongue was like dry cotton. She

was on a bed. White linens. Lights all around. Too bright.

"You're in Anchorage. Sacred Heart Hospital." Drisklay cleared his throat.

She tried turning her head. Couldn't understand why she felt so confined.

"They got you on some pretty strong pain meds," he explained. "You'll be disoriented for a while, but at least you shouldn't hurt."

She tried to wiggle her fingers. Toes. Anything.

"Don't worry. Doctors expect a full recovery." He stood. "Your friend is a lot worse off. Frankly, I didn't expect either of you to survive that kind of crash." He cleared his throat. "Well, it's time for me to sleep off this coffee. I'll check on you again in the morning."

A nurse bustled in and played with the IV lines hooked up to Lacy's arm. Heaviness surrounded her like fog. She shut her eyes and drifted off once more.

***

"So she's ... You say she's going to be ok, though, right?"

Lacy kept her eyes closed. Let the words float around her like a summer breeze.

"Yeah. Once she heals up from the surgery, she should be as good as new."

"How long will that take?"

"Hard to say. As long as she comes off the anesthesia without any problems, she'll move out of intensive care tonight."

"And then where will she go?"

"To the regular floor. Get her strength back. Are you her husband?"

"No, just a friend."

"Well, when she wakes up, I'll tell her you stopped by."

***

Dreams. So many dreams. Kurtis smiling over her, about to nuzzle his nose against hers when his face morphs into Raphael's.

Screaming. Pummeling down in the darkness. Branches scratching at her face. Clawing at her skin. Trying to catch her.

Raphael's unconscious body beside her, staring blankly ahead.

***

The nurse poked her head through Lacy's door. "Someone's here to see you. Are you up for a visitor?"

Lacy winced as she raised the back of her bed to sit up a little. She wiped sweat off her brow. She had been having a bad dream, a nightmare of some sort. She couldn't remember the details.

"Yeah, I'm awake." Her voice sounded groggy. This was her third day post-surgery. Or was it her fourth? She had a hard time keeping track of time. She knew Kurtis wasn't coming back until the weekend, though, and Drisklay had flown home to the East Coast. Was it Raphael, then? Nobody had told her anything about him, where he was, how he was recovering.

If he was recovering.

"Oh, my little baby, it's been so long since I've seen you."

Lacy bit her lip as Sandy bustled into the room, rushed to her bedside, and clasped her hand. "Oh, my little sweetheart, so much has happened to you." And right then and there, before Lacy could ask a single question, her foster mom started to pray.

"Oh, precious heavenly Father, I love you so much. I love you for saving my sweet Lacy's life. I love you for protecting her from the men who were trying to hurt her. I love you so much, Lord, and I pray you would fill my sweet little girl with

121

so much joy and peace and healing that she would be wrapped up in your arms from this moment on until she leaves this hospital, even stronger than she was before."

Sandy went on longer, but Lacy was too disoriented to pay much attention.

"How did you know I was here?" she asked when Sandy was done.

"Your friend called. The nice policemen. Kurtis, I think his name was. He called me and Carl, filled us in on what happened. I'm sorry I wasn't here sooner, sweetie. It took us a couple days to get everything figured out, you know, get the tickets, make all the arrangements." She shook her head and clucked her tongue. "Just look at you. I hope you'll forgive me. I wanted to be here sooner, really I did."

Lacy was about to respond, but Sandy was still talking. "It's just eating your father up inside that he couldn't come, too, so he made me promise to give him updates night and day on how you're improving. You look so beautiful, sweetie. All grown up. You've let your hair grow out. It's so much nicer that way."

Lacy wanted to laugh, which was just as painful for her incision site as crying. "I can't believe you're here," was all she could say.

"And I'll be here as long as you need, sweetie. Well, at least a week, and after that we'll just have to see how things are going, because you know Carl. He's just a mess when there's nobody there to cook and clean and make sure he gets on a matching tie before he preaches. But you know I'm gonna be here for you, precious. That's why I came as fast as I could."

She took Lacy's hand and kissed it. "I'm just so happy. It's such a relief to see you. It could have been a lot worse. Raphael, he's not doing well from what I can gather. I asked them, you know, while they were showing me to your room, but of course it's hard to get any real information. But that could have been you, darling. Your policeman friend said they caught the man, the one chasing you. He won't be troubling you anymore. Now, I don't think Drisklay would agree to it, but you know you can always come home and live with us if you ever need." A spry smile stretched across her face. "But from the sound of it, I wonder if that policeman friend of yours has other plans. Maybe?"

"He's a trooper," Lacy corrected.

Sandy took a deep breath. "Well, now, you just sit tight and get your rest, and I'm going to find me a bathroom, because I got off the plane and took a cab right here I was so anxious to see you. But now that I know you're ok, I've really got some business to tend to. I won't be long, darling. Don't worry about a thing."

She swept out of the room, but even after she left, a warm, loving presence remained wrapped around Lacy's body, filling her with a peace she hadn't experienced in four lonely years.

CHAPTER 17

The nurse handed Lacy a slip of paper. "Here's the prescription for your pain meds. You can stop by any pharmacy and get them filled."

"I'll take care of that for you, hon." Sandy reached out and took the form. "She probably shouldn't take them on an empty stomach, either. Right?"

The nurse shrugged. "I guess not."

Lacy was ready to go outside, to enjoy the fresh air once more.

"Doctor Jacobson wants you to check up with your general provider in a week. Do you need us to help make you an appointment?"

"Do you have a doctor in Anchorage, sweetie?" Sandy asked, as if Lacy needed a translator. She lowered her voice. "Do you have insurance? Because Carl and I can help with the medical bills, you know."

"It's all right," Lacy insisted. Money had been tight

working at the daycare, but at least her pitiful pay qualified her for state health insurance, so her entire hospitalization would be covered. That was one perk of getting transplanted into an oil-rich state.

The nurse made a little mark on her clipboard. "Well, if you don't have any other questions for me, you're free to head home."

Lacy forced a smile, even though the word *home* stabbed at her heart like a giant icicle. "Thank you."

"Oh, one more thing," Sandy inserted. "Is she supposed to be taking baths or showers or just leaving the area dry or what?"

"I'd stick with sponge baths until you see your doctor in a week," the nurse replied.

Lacy felt like apologizing for her mom. "Thank you," she repeated, hoping Sandy didn't have any other questions.

The nurse nodded. "Just let the charge nurse at the front desk know when you leave."

"Are you sure she should walk? Don't you have a wheelchair she can use or something?"

The nurse raised an eyebrow. "Do you want a wheelchair?"

"I'm all right," Lacy answered.

"Are you sure?" Sandy pressed. "You just had a major surgery, and, well, I hate to say it, but you look like you've been in a fight or something. Wait, Raphael never hit you, did he? I didn't want to say it when you two were so close, but I always had a bad feeling about him."

Lacy shook her head. She had been so happy to see Sandy she forgot how smothered her foster mom could make her feel.

Sandy held onto her arm while they made their way to the exit. "Carl said it would be all right for me to rent a car for the day while we settle in. I've checked us into a little missionary house that belongs to an old seminary friend of his. They're not charging us, which is awful sweet of them."

Once outside, Sandy handed her ticket to the parking valet. "Could you be careful, sir?" she asked, "It's a rental."

They sat down on a bench to wait. Lacy's mind was still reeling, replaying all the details of the past few days so her doped-up mind wouldn't mix them up. The man in the Dodge, the one who followed Raphael to Alaska, was behind bars. By all appearances, he was the last link to the murder on the North End pier. It should be good news. Great news. Except it was clouded by the fact that Raphael was still in critical condition. Nobody could guess if he'd pull through. Lacy had wanted to see him once she was well enough to walk, but the nurses said he was refusing visitors. Was that it, then? Was that how their whole tragic story was going to end?

The valet arrived with the rental, and Sandy insisted on holding Lacy's arm to the car and buckling her once she got in. "The mission house should only be ten minutes away. If I don't lose our way before then," she added with a grin.

Lacy adjusted the seat belt strap so it wasn't pressed against her incision site. Sandy got lost within two turns of the hospital but filled the extra driving time prattling on about grandchildren and foster kids Lacy hadn't thought of in years, some she had never met. Her mind zoomed in and out of the conversation, either from the exhaustion or the pain meds or a combination of both.

Half an hour after they left the hospital, Sandy's phone rang. "I'm a block or two away," she answered, "if I got my directions right. Sorry for making you wait ... Yup, I'll see you soon." She hung up the phone and turned down a cul-de-sac in a small neighborhood full of duplex-style houses.

"Who was that?" Lacy asked and then saw her old car parked in one of the driveways. She also recognized the man getting out of the front seat.

"Did I forget to mention it?" Sandy replied with a massive grin. "We're having company."

CHAPTER 18

Lacy couldn't read Kurtis's expression when he opened the door to help her out of Sandy's rental.

"You ok?" he asked quietly.

She was still trying absorb the fact that these two people from her very distinct and very disconnected lives were both staring at her, studying her reaction.

"How do you feel?"

She didn't know how to answer him. Part of her wanted to feign illness and hide in bed for the rest of the day.

Kurtis took one arm and Sandy another, and they led her up the porch steps to the mission home. Sandy reached into a hanging basket and grabbed a key. Once inside, she put down her bag and yawned. "You two get comfortable. I've got to rest for a minute."

Kurtis shut the front door. "Should we head to the couch?"

Lacy felt even more awkward than she had the first time Madeline caught them snuggling together at Kurtis's house.

"Where's the munchkin?" she asked.

"She's at the daycare now. Kim will take her back to her place at the end of the day. I'm not staying long. I just came to drop off your car." He cleared his throat. "And see how you're doing, of course."

"So Sandy called you?"

"I called her, actually. I figured you'd want her to know about the accident. And then she just stayed in touch whether I wanted her to or not." He let out a little laugh.

"I hope she didn't bug you too much or anything."

"No." His good-humored smile was back. She had missed that. Kurtis adjusted in the couch so his leg was close to hers without actually touching it. "She said you were leaving the hospital, and I had the day off, and well, I figured you'd want your car back."

"You didn't have to, you know." Lacy tried to read any hidden meaning behind this visit. He could have held onto the car. Could have kept it in Glennallen so she'd have a reason to go back once she recovered.

"No problem. My buddy Taylor is heading back from town today, so it worked out perfect. I'll just catch a ride home with him. Your car's fine, by the way. Whoever was after you, looks like he unhooked the alternator, that's all. Sucked your battery dry, but we got it up and going just fine. Made it all the way to town today with no problems." He flashed a grin. "And I changed your oil, too."

"Thank you for everything." She had a hard time meeting his eyes.

"Don't mention it."

She didn't know what else to say. Soon, they would have to talk. A lot. About the past. About Raphael. And then about the future.

It was a conversation she dreaded more than just about anything.

"Listen," she said, "I'm really sorry about …"

"Shh." He put his arm around the back of the couch, careful not to touch her. "You don't need to worry about that right now."

"But if I hadn't …"

"Let's just save all that for later, ok?" There was that compassionate look in his eyes again. How could she have taken him for granted for so long?

Something in Kurtis's pocket beeped, and he took out his phone.

"It's Taylor," he said. "He's outside waiting for me."

"That was fast."

The same warm expression. The same soft glance.

She realized then she didn't want him to go. "When are you coming back to town?"

The hint of a smile. "I have next Thursday off."

"Good," Sandy shouted from down the hall. "She'll need a ride to the doctor's office. Want to volunteer?"

Lacy looked for a place to hide her face, but Kurtis only chuckled. "I can take you to your appointment." He leveled his eyes. "If that's all right with you."

She didn't know what to say. Her life, her relationships were all in limbo while she waited to hear about Raphael. Was he recovering? Would he even survive? He wasn't answering his phone calls or text messages, and the doctors refused give her any real information.

Stupid patient privacy laws.

Now, here was Kurtis, the same sweet, steadfast Kurtis who had been so good to her. Watching her attentively. Waiting for her response.

"That would be fine," she answered.

He let out a sigh. Was there more to be said?

Not here. Not now.

But when?

He walked to the door. "Coffee afterwards?" he asked.

Gentle. Hopeful.

"Good idea," Sandy called out.

Lacy let out a choppy breath. "Maybe if I'm feeling well enough by then." She couldn't take her eyes off Kurtis. What had happened to them?

"I guess I'll see you Thursday then." He turned the knob and was gone.

CHAPTER 19

"So, you heard from that nice policeman lately?" Sandy asked as she folded laundry at the Anchorage mission house.

"He's a trooper." Lacy had forgotten how many times she'd corrected her mother in the past few days.

"I still don't see what the difference is." Sandy put one of the pans away. "Well, have you heard from this *trooper* friend of yours lately?"

Lacy rolled her eyes. She was so glad to see Sandy, to be in the same house, to talk about the past without having to remember all the lies of her cover story. But still, there was only so much smothering a New England girl could take.

Sandy folded one of her floral skirts. "Well, if you don't want me prying around in your love life, I can respect that."

"It's not that." She didn't want to shut Sandy out. God knew she needed someone she could turn to for advice right about now.

Sandy put down the blouse she'd been folding and sat

down on the couch. "Then what is it, sweetheart?"

Lacy let out her breath. She knew her mom liked Kurtis. Of course she would. Kurtis was polite, attentive, respectful. He had been thoughtful enough to call Sandy to let her know about the accident. But there were some things her foster mom didn't understand.

"I don't know." Lacy stared over the top of Sandy's shoulder to avoid making eye contact. "There's so much going on right now."

Sandy grinned. "Like the fact that an Alaska state *trooper* bought you an engagement ring? Remind me again, was that before or after he saved your life in the car crash?"

"He's not the one making things confusing. It's …" She let her voice trail off.

"It's Raphael," Sandy finished for her.

Lacy studied her fingernail and nodded.

"You still have feelings for him?"

Lacy's spine tingled at the hint of incredulity she detected in Sandy's tone. Why shouldn't she still have feelings for him? He was her first love. The first man she ever imagined spending the rest of her life with. The first man besides her foster dad she had ever trusted.

Sandy leaned forward on the couch. "You know I'm only

looking out for you, honey, don't you?"

Lacy stared at the pile of clothes.

"Come on," Sandy pressed. "What's going on? You can talk to me. We could always talk things through."

But that was before, Lacy wanted to point out. Before Raphael made his boneheaded mistake and got them mixed up in some Mafia drama that stripped Lacy of her identity, her entire life. Four years lost. Completely wasted.

So why was she mad at Sandy and not at Raphael?

Lacy shook her head. "Everything is so confusing."

"That's perfectly understandable, dear. You've been through so much. And now there are two men in the picture, and you don't know what you're going to do, but any choice is bound to hurt at least one of them. Is that it?"

Lacy swallowed past the lump in her throat. "Yeah," she croaked.

Sandy nodded and tucked a strand of hair into her braid. "I understand entirely."

Lacy knew her mom was just being polite. What would Sandy know about it? What would she know about mourning a lost love for four years only to find he was really alive? What would she know about being close to a strong, protective man who'd never met the real you? When had Sandy ever been split, torn between two lives, two loves, two identities?

"You know I adore Carl," Sandy said. "He and I are every bit as much in love today as we were on our wedding day. Even more so, actually."

Lacy nodded. Living with Carl and Sandy was the first proof she'd had that happy marriages weren't simply lies Hollywood rom-coms tried to sell.

Sandy leaned back on the couch and crossed her arms, so Lacy knew this would be a long story.

"Before I met Carl, I was going steady with a young man from my father's church. He had just finished medical school and wanted me to move with him to Alabama. He was kind. Considerate. Polite. From a well-off family, nice folks in their Southern mansion, the package deal."

Sandy adjusted her French braid over her shoulder. "My parents adored him. Our families adored each other, really, which is part of the reason why both David and I felt so comfortable in our relationship. He was a few years older than me, but what did that matter? When he asked me to move to Alabama with him, my parents couldn't understand why I didn't start packing that same day. There was just this gut feeling, though, this premonition that if I moved with David away from home, away from both our families, we'd lose ninety percent of the things that made our relationship so perfect. Does that make sense?"

Lacy nodded.

"But my mom really wanted me to go, and I didn't want to be alone. So I transferred from UVA to Alabama to be with him while he was doing his residency. Do you have any idea how hard hospitals make those residents work?"

Lacy didn't want to break the flow of Sandy's story by answering.

"He was so busy, I'd sneak to the hospital once or twice a week, drop off a snack or little note or something, try to keep him well fed and encouraged. Other than that, we went a whole semester hardly seeing each other. It was a lonely time for me."

Lacy bit her lip. Unless Sandy went four years living the life of a perfect stranger, forbidden from speaking to anyone from her past, Lacy doubted she knew the real meaning of loneliness. But maybe that wasn't fair, either. It couldn't have been easy for her mom back then, away from home, away from her family …

"And that's when I met Carl." A slow smile spread across Sandy's face, and Lacy instinctively grinned back.

"Carl was basically everything David wasn't. He came from a broken home, no family name, no money. And of course, you had the race issue." She chuckled to herself. "I tried for three months to work up the nerve to tell my parents."

"What did they say?" Lacy asked.

"Nothing. I always chickened out. I let little bits leak out. Told them how busy David was, how I wasn't so sure anymore I wanted to marry a doctor if he was going to be so tied up with his patients I'd only get five minutes of his time. And finally, my mom read enough between the lines to realize there was another man involved. I'm sure she was disappointed, but she was reasonable. She said she wanted me happy. Said if David wasn't the one for me, she just wanted to know I was loved and taken care of whoever I ended up with." Another laugh. "That's before she knew Carl was black."

"How'd they find out?" Lacy asked.

"Well, I had to make things official with David first. He knew we were drifting apart, but before I could really give my heart to Carl, I had to tell David everything."

"How'd he take it?"

Sandy let out a sigh. "That wasn't so easy. He understood the part about me breaking up with him because of his schedule. Honestly, I think he was relieved. He'd been feeling guilty that he couldn't give me more time and attention. I mean, he was the one who uprooted me from my home, dragged me to a brand-new state, and then basically forgot I existed. At least, it felt that way sometimes. So in that sense, he understood completely.

"What he couldn't figure out was why I would leave him for Carl. I mean, a black, penniless campus minister who had to go around to churches three months out of every year to beg for his salary — that was a real blow to David's ego, you know? How could I prefer someone like Carl when I could have been with him? But he got over it. Eventually."

"Do you ever talk to him anymore?" Lacy tried to keep her expression neutral, hoping Sandy couldn't perceive the reason for the question.

"Not really. He was an important part of my life for a season. We had fun memories, enjoyed each other's company. In fact, I'm still friends with his mother and sister. Send them Christmas cards every year. But David? Well, we both moved on. He found another girl, they got married, Carl and I eventually moved out of the South, and that was that."

Lacy chose her next words carefully, hoping she wasn't giving too much away. "But do you miss him? I mean, *did* you miss him? Or were things just so good with Carl that ..."

Sandy interrupted with an unlady-like snort. "So good with Carl?" She leaned forward. "Good? Try sitting in a diner for an hour while waitresses walk right by and ignore you and tell me how good that is. Or what about having half your extended family refuse to call you by your married name? You call that good? Or getting your windshield egged. And those are the things I can laugh about now. It got worse. Lots worse. Even the police didn't do much to help. They had this attitude like, *If you didn't want to get regular death threats, lady, why'd you go and marry a colored man?* There was one night I got a call from the hospital. Carl'd been beat up. Attacked by five or six men. Teens, actually. Boys. Do you know what it does to a man's ego to get beat up by thugs nearly half his age? The hospital wanted my permission to donate his organs if he didn't make it, that's how bad it was.

"So if you're asking me if I ever wondered what life would have been like if I'd chosen David instead of Carl, the answer's yes. A hundred times. And I'm not saying a hundred times total. It was more like a hundred times a day, at least during the ugliest spells. Did I wish things were easier like they would have been if I'd married David? Absolutely. But did I regret my decision to choose Carl?"

Lacy leaned forward to hear the answer.

Sandy leveled her eyes. "Never." The word echoed through Lacy's chest, its reverberations falling in sync with her pulse. "Never."

Sandy took up another blouse. Lacy was just going to hang it up in the closet, but Sandy still folded it with perfect creases that could put a clothing store worker to shame. "You thinking about Raphael?" she asked quietly.

Lacy nodded.

Sandy offered a reassuring smile. "Well, I know better than to give you my opinion. If I had listened to my mother, I would have never chosen Carl. Never had the amazing ride we've had. Never met you, our other kids ... That's what would have happened if I'd gone for the safe and easy route."

Safe? Why did it always come back to that? It seemed pretty clear that of the two men, Kurtis was the safe one. Is that what Sandy was talking about? Was she telling her not to settle for safe?

"So you're saying I should be with Raphael?" Lacy asked, wondering if that was even an option anymore. She still hadn't heard from him since the accident. Even once he recovered, Lacy didn't know if she'd learn to trust him again after everything they went through.

"I'm not saying anything of the sort. I don't need to tell you again how I get all nervous and unsettled every time I think of you two together. Now, maybe that's not fair of me. Maybe that's just because you were involved in that incident together so long ago."

Lacy fidgeted with a button on her blouse. She still hadn't told her mom about Raphael's role in the accident at the pier.

Sandy crossed her arms. "Now, I know my mom had her reservations about Carl. Said she didn't understand how I could throw away every chance God had given me for a good life to take such a crazy leap of faith as marry a colored man. I don't think it was flat-out racism on her part. Not totally. A lot of it was her just knowing how hard it would be if we did marry and wanting to protect me from that. I was naïve, see? I thought with all the progress we'd made in the civil rights movement that people would be more accepting. My mom knew better than that and was trying her hardest to look out for me." Sandy adjusted the rose-patterned skirt she was wearing. "Just like I'm trying to do with you. But whatever you choose, if you marry the policeman or give Raphael a chance once he's pulled through his injuries or turn them both down and go have wild adventures somewhere else, I'm giving you my full support. That's something my mom never said to me, and I'm not about to repeat that same mistake."

Lacy offered a weak smile. "Thanks." She was so tired. The pain pills still made her groggy, but she could hardly sleep two or three hours at night before waking up in a clammy, itchy sweat. Maybe it was a side-effect of the medicine. Or maybe it was just her body's way of reacting to her trauma. Either way, she knew she couldn't hold her eyelids open for much longer before she had to lie down for a nap.

Sandy stood and gave Lacy a kiss on the forehead. "You just think about what I said, all right? And don't forget to pray. God will always answer his children when they ask him for wisdom." Sandy paused. "Is that your phone beeping, dear? Do you want me to bring it to you?"

She handed Lacy her cell.

"What is it, sweetheart?" she asked. "Is something wrong?"

Lacy stared at the screen, hardly trusting her eyes. "It's Raphael. He wants me to come see him at the hospital."

CHAPTER 20

Lacy couldn't remember feeling so nervous before. Not during any of her theater auditions or college exams. Not on her first date with Kurtis or the night on the pier when she thought Raphael was going to propose to her.

Sandy pulled Lacy's car into the parking lot of Sacred Heart Hospital. "Take all the time you need, sweetie. I'll just take a walk and give my legs a good stretch."

Lacy nodded. At least Anchorage was smart enough to spray for mosquitoes, so the bugs weren't that unbearable.

Her legs were weak as she took one tentative step after another into the main entrance of Sacred Heart. Her stomach quivered as if her body was afraid she'd be admitted again, operated on, and sent home with meds that turned her brain to fuzz but only took a slight edge off her pain. She knew Raphael's room number but had to ask the volunteer receptionist how to get there.

"That's in C Tower. Third floor. You can take the stairs or

the elevator," the elderly man told her.

She would definitely take the elevator.

When she got to his hallway, her gait slowed even more. The incision site from her surgery throbbed. She took in a deep breath. She could do this.

Whatever you choose, I'm giving you my full support. That was easy for Sandy to say — Sandy, who had made her decision decades earlier. Lacy thought about her mom, torn between a safe man her family loved and a boyfriend who promised adventure. Passion. Danger. She had never imagined Sandy with anyone but Carl. She had turned down the safe man.

Should Lacy? Kurtis was so compassionate. He would understand. She had known Raphael for so many years. Had waited for him for so long. She had never gotten over the pain of losing him, and now that he was back in her life, how could she turn away from him? Especially now, when he faced such a long road to recovery? How could she desert him when he needed her to nurse him? Encourage him?

They had been so great together, she and Raphael. They could look at the same painting and come away with entirely different impressions, but their differences gave them an hour's worth of engaging conversation. They loved the same things — art, theater, Broadway, road trips. The only drives she and

Kurtis took were to Anchorage to fill up on staples at Costco. The most danger she had ever experienced while dating him was traveling over the mountain pass at a conservative forty miles an hour.

But what was wrong with safe? That's the question she had asked herself time and time again. She knew she was still functioning in crisis mode, her brain still reeling from the accident. At some point, she'd have to address what Raphael told her before they crashed. He had made some bad choices. Really bad choices. Choices that cost Lacy four years of her life. How could she be sure he wouldn't repeat the same mistakes again? What if they got married and he did something similar? What if they had a child?

She pictured Kurtis's daughter, so cuddly and headstrong. Lacy would do anything to guard Madeline and only imagined the protective instinct would be stronger once she had a child of her own. How could she forgive herself if she and Raphael had a kid they weren't able to keep safe?

Safe. That same word again. Offering so much comfort, especially after all that Lacy had been through. But so smothering at the same time. The bugs won't bite you if you live in a plastic bubble, but does that count as really living?

She stopped outside Raphael's door and checked the

number three times. Was she ready for this? No. But she was here. Raphael was injured. He needed her. Every other decision could be put on hold until he recovered.

It was the only plan she had as she stepped into the room, but it would have to be enough.

CHAPTER 21

He looked so weak lying on the bed. His arm was in a cast. His face was bruised and covered with cuts, a massive bandage taped over one eye. A nurse adjusted his IV bag and nodded at Lacy.

Raphael glanced over. "What are you doing?" he demanded.

She stopped short of the bed.

"What are you doing?" he repeated. His voice was gravelly, as if each word hurt his throat.

"I came to see you."

"I don't want visitors."

Lacy held her cell in her palm. "You sent me a text." Could she have misread it?

The nurse came around the side of the bed. She put her arm around Lacy's shoulder, walking her a few steps to the door. "His memory's not so good right now," she whispered. "Head trauma."

"Maybe I should come back later."

The nurse shrugged. "It's up to you. He's not the best of company, but maybe seeing someone he knows will do him good. Are you a friend?"

"Yeah. I thought I might cheer him up." How could she have been so wrong?

"You're welcome to try." The nurse pat her arm and slipped out of the room.

Lacy went to Raphael's bed. Her steps were slow. Uncertain.

He didn't look up. "I never texted anyone."

Her throat constricted. "I just wanted to see how you were doing."

"Well, get a good look and tell me what you think."

Lacy knew head injuries could alter personalities. She knew there were tons of medications that could make Raphael so agitated. If there was one thing she had learned from her foster parents, it was that love was unconditional. She tucked the corner of her blouse back into her pants. "I'm glad you're out of the ICU." The cheer in her voice was forced and artificial.

"Makes one of us."

She took a deep breath, trying to remember all the good

qualities that had made her fall in love with Raphael in the first place. "I've been waiting to hear how you've been doing."

He didn't look at her. "Just peachy. Can't you tell?"

"I'm sorry this happened," she whispered, wondering if saying so would only make him angrier. For some reason, it all felt like her fault. The car chase. The crash. His injuries.

"No worse than what I deserve," he mumbled.

She took a step closer. "Don't think that way. You're not the one running people off the road ..."

"I led them right to you." His voice was suddenly stronger. "Don't you realize that, Lace? Can't you put the pieces together? I led them right to you."

"You had no way to know you'd find me in Alaska."

He let out a mirthless laugh. "I always knew you were trusting. I didn't think you were stupid, too."

Why was he saying this? Why was he acting this way?

"I came to Alaska because the Mafia put me up to it." For the first time, he looked right at her. His eyes were dark, like angry storm clouds. "Are you getting the full picture now?"

She hoped he didn't notice the way her lips trembled.

"They told me they'd kill me if I didn't help them get to you. Threatened my parents and brother. They said if I didn't help find you, they'd go after Carl and Sandy, too. I had to try something. Carl had told me about the phone call from the trooper in Glennallen. That's how I knew where you were. The biking tour, the life-long dream of coming to Alaska, it was all a lie."

Her world was spinning. She needed a cup of water. Where was that nurse?

He shook his head. "I may as well have killed you myself and saved the Mafia the effort."

She was weak. Hardly able to stand. She was so dizzy she couldn't focus on him. He was talking like a lunatic. Was it the medicine? Why had the nurse left her alone with him? Somebody would come check on them soon. Explain again how this was all the side-effects of the drugs. That had to be the reason, right?

"It wasn't your fault." She wasn't sure which of them she was trying to convince.

He let out his breath in a frustrated huff. "Have you been listening to anything I said? Geeze, Lace, get it through your skull. I brought these men to you. I practically held the gun to your head for them."

"Why?" Her voice trembled. She glanced at the door. Suddenly, safe was a word that sounded a whole lot more inviting.

"I didn't have the heart to tell you everything at first, couldn't scare you away. So I tampered with your car, made sure you couldn't make it to Anchorage without me. I was gonna tell you everything on the road. We had to get out of Alaska, start over somewhere else. I thought we had enough of a head start on them. I thought I could drive us to Canada, get lost with you there. But I just dragged you into even more danger. I should have finished everything off in Massachusetts. I should have known they'd follow me here."

It wasn't true. It couldn't be. "But it wasn't your fault," she insisted again as a gunshot ripped through the air, shattering her eardrums.

CHAPTER 22

She was frozen. Paralyzed. Somewhere in the back of her head, she felt her vocal cords screaming but wasn't sure if the sound came out or not. Her ears buzzed. Swarms of angry, high-pitched mosquitoes.

"Get down." Raphael's voice was garbled, as if he were talking under water. Her vision was blurry. Like watching a scratched DVD where everything appears in freeze frames.

Raphael's hand on her shoulder. Stronger than she would have guessed. Pushing her to the ground. She hit her hip on the floor. Banged her head on the hospital bed. Shouldn't she feel the pain?

Another gun shot. Why did they have to be so loud? A scream. Raphael's scream. She had never heard a person make that noise.

Drops of blood splattered on her blouse. Was she injured? She couldn't feel anything. Had her entire nervous system shut down?

She crouched low, certain the attacker would keep shooting. She wondered how small she could make her body, envisioned turning herself into nothing but a speck. A dot.

Shouting. Curses coming from the doorway. Was there more than one of them, then? Another shot. This time, Lacy heard herself scream. Ear-grating. Soul-piercing scream.

Terrified voices in the hallway. Her mind projecting the image of the shooter into her brain even though her eyes were squeezed tight.

"Get him out of here." An authoritative voice. Strong. In control. Someone she could trust.

"Check on the patient." Scared. She never knew so much fear could be packed into a single phrase.

"He's been shot."

A nervous bustle all around her. Lacy stayed crouched in place.

"Got his artery."

More uneasy exchanges. Shouted orders.

Raphael's hand stretching out for her. Reaching down from the hospital bed. "I'm so sorry, Lace."

A worried nurse. "Shh. We're gonna try to get you through this."

"Where is she?" That strong voice again. Stable. Safe.

"Jo?"

She couldn't answer. Couldn't open her eyes. But it didn't matter. He found her. Dropped by her side and wrapped her up in his arms.

"Are you ok?" Kurtis. Why was he here? How had he known where she was? "Are you hurt?"

"I don't know."

He ran his hands over her. It wasn't until she felt his sturdiness that she realized she was shaking.

"You're ok," he finally breathed and hugged her once more, resting his cheek on the top of her head. "You're safe now."

CHAPTER 23

Hours after the shooting, Lacy was still trembling. Two officers had driven her to the Anchorage police department. They didn't tell her what she was waiting for, but she had a pretty good idea.

They settled her in a room they assured her was completely secure. It was cold and drafty, with a dank, almost mildewy smell. A female officer asked her a few questions about the shooting, quickly realized Lacy was too stunned to offer any helpful information, and then left her alone with a cup of orange juice and half a jumbo Costco muffin.

She didn't realize someone was watching her from another room until she took out her cell to call Sandy and a loud, projected voice shattered the silence. "No phone calls, miss. It's for your own safety."

She put the phone on the table in front of her.

Secure. The officers told her she was secure, but that was a far cry from feeling safe.

She was cold. Could she ask for a blanket? Why had that woman just left her with tepid juice and an old snack? Lacy had so many questions. Was Raphael ok? How had Kurtis shown up? And why? Who was the shooter and what happened to him? Had anybody thought to explain to Sandy what was going on, or was she still waiting at the hospital, wondering what was taking so long?

She hated being cooped up in here. Cooped up with nothing but questions. She tried to squeeze her eyes shut, but all she could see was Raphael's blood staining her blouse. Why hadn't the police offered her a change of clothes? Couldn't they see how filthy she was?

A knock on the door. Lacy stood up from her metal folding chair.

"You in here, Jo? It's me."

Relief rushed over her like an avalanche at the sound of Kurtis's voice. She flung the door open. "What's going on? Where's Sandy? Is Raphael hurt? Why are they keeping me locked up in here?" She rattled off each question without pausing for breath.

He frowned. "Are you sure you want to hear everything right now?"

She bit her lip and nodded. It was like waiting for an

injection you knew would hurt, but the anticipation was worse than the shot itself.

"Ok." Kurtis sat in another fold-up chair beside her. "So, to start off, yes, Raphael was hurt. It's …" He lowered his voice. "It's pretty bad. They're doing what they can, but nobody seems too hopeful."

She wanted to tell him. Tell him how Raphael pushed her down out of the way of the bullet, but she couldn't find her voice.

"And they brought you here because we got the one shooter, he's in custody, but nobody knows if there were others, too. So they're gonna keep you here until Drisklay …" His voice caught. He cleared his throat. "Drisklay's on his way right now."

She had expected that much. Expected it and feared it, too. Lacy couldn't meet his eyes. "Does Sandy know?"

He swallowed and nodded. "Yeah. I told her everything. She's grabbing a few things for you, and then she'll be over. It'll be her turn next."

"Her turn?" The pronouncement sounded ominous. "Her turn for what?"

He stared at his knees. "To say good-bye."

The words hung in the air between them, filling the heavy

spaces. It was so dense, Lacy wondered how either of them were still breathing.

So this was it. Lacy had been so ready to be rid of Jo, ready to slip out of her old identity just like she was ready to change out of her bloody blouse. But not like this.

Drisklay was coming. That could only mean one thing. A new placement. Except this time, Lacy couldn't argue with him about whether or not it was necessary.

She sighed and shut her eyes. She knew there would be no tears. Not today. Not tomorrow. They probably wouldn't fall for a month. Maybe two. She'd be driving somewhere with her new driver's license, listening to the radio station in a new town on her way to her new job, and a song would come on. Something that would remind her of Kurtis. Raphael. Sandy. Everything that had happened to her. That's when she would cry.

Then and not before. Betrayed by her own body, which felt some primitive need to conserve energy in this time of crisis instead of offering her the immediate release she craved.

"How did you find me?" she asked. "How did you know I was in trouble?"

"Something had been bugging me since the accident," Kurtis explained. "Your car, somebody tampered with it. Somebody in Glennallen. But the Dodge that was chasing you was coming from the other way. So I got to thinking, and all I could figure was Raphael had done it. Maybe he wasn't who you thought he was. Then Drisklay got in touch, said he was worried because you weren't returning his calls."

"I thought he was just trying to get me to go back to Glennallen."

"He was trying to keep you alive," Kurtis corrected her. "And then I told him what I'd figured about the car, and he said it was suspicious enough that we should look into it. So he made plans to fly back here, and I dropped Madeline off at the daycare with Kim and drove down myself. I called Sandy when I got to town and asked where you were. She said you went to the hospital to visit Raphael, and ..."

"It wasn't his fault, you know." Lacy wasn't sure why she said it. She just couldn't stand the way Kurtis spoke his name. "I mean, he was involved, but he wasn't trying to hurt me or anything." Was that true? Or was she just making excuses?

"He should have thought of that before getting you mixed up in any of this." Kurtis let out his breath. "I mean, I understand you two have a past together, but seriously ..."

Couldn't they talk about something else? Anything else?

He frowned. "If he wanted what was best for you, he should have thought enough to stay away. He should have ..."

He waved his hand in the air. "Never mind."

She was glad when he dropped the matter. "So did Drisklay say anything about where I'll be going from here?" she asked.

Kurtis's hard-set expression softened. "You know he can't tell me that sort of thing."

She nodded. "Yeah. I know. I just thought, with you being a cop and all ..."

"I'm a trooper, remember?" He forced a smile.

Lacy couldn't return it.

"I need to go soon. Got a long drive home." He stood up. "I'm just glad you're going to be safe. Finally."

He took a step toward the door, and Lacy realized in that moment what a fool she'd been. A fool to let her memories of Raphael tarnish her relationship with Kurtis in the first place. A fool to turn down Kurtis when all he'd ever wanted to do was keep her happy. Safe. A fool to have spent so much energy wondering if she could really settle down with someone like him.

Now, it was too late. This was good-bye. This wasn't a boyfriend and girlfriend taking time off to step back and evaluate their relationship. This wasn't getting dumped, hoping one day your ex might regret it and realize what a horrible mistake he'd made.

This was good-bye. Just as final as if one of them had died.

They could have been so good together …

"I'll miss you." She stood and took a step toward him.

"Me, too." His voice was tight as he opened his arms.

What else was there to say? It wasn't as if Lacy were moving to go to college or study abroad where she could write or call whenever she missed him. She couldn't promise to let him know when she arrived safely at her destination. Neither of them knew where she was going.

That's the way it had to be.

Their hug was awkward at first, like two partners at a junior high dance. Then he rested his cheek on the top of her head, and she felt the rise of his chest as he inhaled. He ran his thumb across her cheek. She looked up at him. His lips were so close. So kissable. She shut her eyes as one of his tears dripped onto her face.

"Good-bye." He stepped back. Lacy watched him leave, listened to the hollow sound of the door as it clicked and locked in place behind him.

CHAPTER 24

The silence was haunting. Heavy. Relentless. Icicles of loneliness weighing down on her heart. Why had she let any of this happen? She should have never gotten in the car with Raphael last week. Never left Glennallen.

But then what? Wait to get killed by the man who followed him to Alaska?

Raphael. She would never see him again. She knew it just as plainly as if he had died from his injuries. Maybe he would die. Lacy saw the next few weeks stretch lifelessly before her. Checking the Alaska Daily News website, constantly reloading to see if there was any information of his passing. Would the media find it newsworthy enough to report? Would anybody else in the entire blasted state care? Would she ever know what happened to him?

She had been mad at God, angry at him for forcing her to choose between two men. She had grumbled. Complained. Now, he was taking both Kurtis and Raphael away from her.

That should teach her for whining so much. Why couldn't she have been content? Content working at the daycare, staying in Glennallen. The Fourth of July salmon feed was only a week away. She could have been engaged. Married Kurtis. Adopted Madeline. Added a few more kids to their family. Two weeks ago, that sort of a future seemed so confining. Restricting.

Lacy would do just about anything now to reverse the clock and change what had happened. Stop Raphael from coming to Alaska in the first place. She didn't hate him for what he'd done. It was his fault, but she couldn't hate him. She didn't love him either, though, not like she had in the past. She loved his memory, wished it weren't tainted by all the horrible mistakes he'd made. But she was no longer in love with him.

Maybe she had grown up in the past week.

Maybe she had become more like Jo than she originally realized.

She was hungry. Weak from the trauma of the day. The trauma of the past four years, really. How much could one person endure? *"For I know the plans I have for you."* Was this some cosmic version of a practical joke or something?

Raphael had found peace in religion. Solace. He threw himself into his new zeal for Christianity the same way he pursued his art. The same way he pursued Lacy. He wore his faith on his sleeve but still kept on making one dumb choice after another. No overdose of spiritual fervor could offset his immaturity.

She thought about Kurtis, how she felt comfortable if he mentioned God and just as comfortable if he didn't. He lived out his faith instead of parroting fancy church phrases, instead of thrusting his religion on anyone with a strong enough stomach to listen.

"For I know the plans I have for you." Lacy wondered if God really did have a plan for each person's life, or if it was more like a Choose Your Own Adventure story, where he knew all the possible outcomes but let everyone flounder around on their own to figure everything out.

Oh well. There was no use dwelling on any of this. What would it help?

The door burst open, and Lacy didn't experience the repugnance she usually felt at Drisklay's appearance. This wasn't his fault, either. After Lacy had made such a big fuss about no longer needing his protection, he was here again, ready to whisk her away to someplace safe. She should feel grateful. Instead, she felt nothing.

Empty.

Like a black winter sky when clouds cover all the stars.

He took a sip from his Styrofoam cup. "Jo."

She had spent so many years hating that name, that identity. She had been a fool.

He set his cup down, splashing a few drops of cold coffee on the table between them. "I didn't expect to be back in Alaska so soon."

She waited. Waited for his lecture about how dumb she had been to resume a relationship with someone from her past. Complain about how her and Raphael's stupidity cost the program so many thousands of dollars for their new relocations. Remind her how crucially important it was to stick to the directives. Obey the rules. Never trust anybody. Never let anybody come close to learning about her past. Instead, he sat down with a groan. "You've had an eventful day." He folded his hands on the table. "So, let me tell you what's gonna happen from here."

Lacy refused to think back to the night four years ago when she first met Drisklay and had a very similar conversation. She was a different person now. Older. Hopefully wiser. Whatever was going to happen to her, she would accept it like a mature adult. Drisklay was trying to help her, and she was going to jump through whatever hoops he laid out for her without complaining. Her life and future depended on it.

She nodded. "I'm ready."

CHAPTER 25

Drisklay's briefing was just as long and involved as his first one had been back in Massachusetts. Apparently, he had an entire twenty-minute speech memorized where he talked about all the dangers that might befall a protectee who leaves the program. Scare tactics, really. Except Lacy didn't need those anymore. She had already been terrified into compliance.

Her next stop would be to a safe house out of state. Drisklay didn't tell her where it was, just told her she'd fly out with him in a few hours. She'd wait there for a week or two, however long it took the department to put together her new cover identity. She listened to it all as if she were a distant observer. A member of the audience watching a crime drama in a theater. Maybe a new minimalist musical.

Definitely not a comedy.

"Do you have any questions for me?" Drisklay asked, tipping his cup back to take in the last few drops of coffee.

She licked her lips. "How's …" Drisklay had been talking

for so long, she couldn't trust her voice. "How's Raphael?

He frowned. "He took a lot of chances. You know there's no way we can guarantee safety for someone like that."

That wasn't good enough. She'd spent four years wondering what had really happened to him that night at the North End. Even though she knew there was never going to be a future where she and Raphael ended up together, she refused to step into the next act of her life without knowing the full truth.

"What did the doctors say?" She tried to make her voice sound forceful but wasn't sure she pulled it off.

Drisklay stared at his empty cup. "He didn't make it. Too much blood loss."

Lacy let his answer float in the air around her. Took in the truth a small breath at a time. *He didn't make it.*

Drisklay made a move as if he were going to drink again but changed his mind. "I'm sorry."

Didn't make it.

Lacy knew at some point the realization would hit her full in the gut. Maybe on the plane with Drisklay, or maybe once she got settled in her new home in the Lower 48. All the sorrow, the grieving, the regrets — that would all come.

Later.

Now, she had a plane to catch. A safe house to reach. She

hoped wherever they took her at least had some good movies. Her brain could use some mindless numbing.

"Well." Drisklay stood. "I have a few details to oversee before we head to the airport. In the meantime, I think there was somebody who …"

The moment he cracked the door open, Sandy shouldered her way in. She was carrying a backpack, a small duffel, and several shopping bags. "I'm here, sweetie."

Drisklay squeezed past all the luggage and shut the door behind him. Sandy set the bags on the floor and hurried toward Lacy. They hugged. Lacy did what she could to mentally record the feeling of her mom's hands around her back, wondering how long until the memory faded and dissolved.

"I'm sorry," Sandy sniffed, laughing at herself. "I promised myself I'd be the strong one here." She tilted her head and pouted at Lacy. Mascara dribbled down her cheeks. "I brought your stuff." She gestured toward the bags. "That's the backpack and duffel you had at the mission home. And I went to the store to grab some other things." She pulled various items out of the shopping bags. New socks. A few cute hair accessories. Tampons and deodorant. "I got a couple books, too. I don't know what you like to read these days, so I just picked out some that looked interesting. I didn't know how long you'd be on your flight or …" She let her voice trail off.

"Thanks," Lacy mumbled.

Her mom sniffed loudly. "I'm so sorry all this happened, dear."

"I know."

"Some people would say something like *Everything happens for a reason*, or *God won't give you more than you can handle*. But the truth is, God gives his people things they can't handle every single day. It's not fair. It's not pleasant. It's just life." She sat in the folding chair, and Lacy caught a whiff of fabric softener wafting from the folds of her skirt. Could she remember that smell always?

"God is good," Sandy continued. "We can't ever doubt that. And his Word tells us he'll work things out for our good if we love him. But that doesn't keep bad things from happening. All these horrible events that have happened to you, those are bad. Still, we got to hold faith that God knows what he's doing. He can make good come from all these tragedies. He *will* if you trust him." She sighed. "I wish I could tell you more, sweetie. Wish I could give you all the answers. But here I am, hardly a crumb of wisdom to my name, and you're probably starving for a whole loaf right about now."

"It would be nice," Lacy admitted. They talked a little

more. Lacy explained about how Kurtis grew suspicious about the car and drove down to Anchorage to check on her. How Raphael had been involved with everything from the start. How surprised Lacy was to feel so little at the news of his death.

"That's because it hasn't sunk in, sweetheart," Sandy explained. "You see, God knows that some things are easier to take in little by little. Bite-sized chunks, if you will. Now, I know Raphael did you wrong, and I bet you feel like you should be angry with him. The fact is, you probably will be. That's just a part of grieving, darling. And don't you think that just because he's the one who put you in all that danger that you shouldn't mourn for him. I'd be worried over you if you didn't. That boy was important to you. I remember you two together back in Boston. You had a chemistry. A bond. Might not have been the wisest or most godly of bonds, but that don't matter right now. What matters is he's gone, and eventually you're going to have to process all that. Cry as much as you need. Nothing cleanses the soul like prayer and a good sob. And don't feel pressured to get over him too soon either, hon. That's the other mistake some folks make. Don't rush the grieving period. I always like to picture my tears are the rain that's gonna water the flowers God's sending my way. He does that, you know, makes beauty out of our sorrow. Sometimes it takes longer than others. That's why we need to ask him for patience."

She reached out and stroked Lacy's cheek as Drisklay's voice carried into their room from the intercom. "Five more minutes, then we got a plane to catch."

Sandy wrapped her arms around Lacy. "I pray for you every single day."

Lacy wished she knew how to respond.

"Is there anything you want me to tell your dad?"

Lacy took in a deep breath. "Just tell him not to worry about me. Tell him ..." She faltered once before finding her voice again. "Just tell him I'm safe, and I love him a lot."

"We both love you." Sandy held her even tighter. She wiped her eyes. "I know this has to happen, sweetie. It's for your own safety, but it's just so hard."

Lacy nodded.

"Now one more thing," Sandy went on. "Let's say down the road you meet some nice young man. Someone like that trooper friend of yours who wants to marry you. As long as he loves you and he's a believer, you both have our blessing. Ok? He doesn't need to dig around and investigate and call Carl out of the blue this time. Got it?"

Lacy tried to laugh along with her mom but couldn't.

Sandy's whole body sighed as they held each other for the

last time. "I know I can't ask you anything about where you're going, and maybe you don't know yet either. But wherever the good Lord takes you, honey, my prayer for you is that you'll realize how much he loves you. Wherever you are. Whatever heartaches you've had to suffer. His love for you is greater than all of that. So you draw close to God, sweetie, and when you're praying to him, feeling his big, powerful arms wrapping around you and holding you tight and keeping you safe, you remember your daddy and me are praying for you awful fierce. Those times you feel the Holy Spirit right there with you, comforting you, that's gonna be God answering our prayers and showing you how much you're loved."

Lacy bit her lip. Maybe she could find those tears today after all.

Sandy took in a deep breath. "Now, I'm not gonna say good-bye, because good-byes are for people who don't know Jesus and don't have the hope we do that one day we'll all be together again. You just hang on 'til then, sweet thing. Brighter times are coming your way. I just know it."

She kissed Lacy's cheek and with a flourish of her long French braid and rustling floral skirt, she was gone.

CHAPTER 26 – *one week later*

Tired. Lacy was so tired. Tired of the Texas heat. The safe house had air conditioning, but it hardly made any difference. The whole town had gathered for their little Fourth of July parade two blocks over. She had listened all morning to bagpipers warming up across the street.

She had forgotten how many movies she'd watched since Drisklay dumped her out here. She'd breezed through all the historical and romance novels Sandy bought, even though none of them had really interested her. Sometimes she wondered if this was what certain believers imagined purgatory would be like. A lot of waiting. Some sorrow. Disappointment. Occasional anger. Fear. Loneliness.

And not a whole lot else.

Lacy sat on the safe house couch with her legs tucked beneath her. Drisklay had taken her phone so she couldn't access her Bible app, but Lacy had found a worn New King James Bible on a bookshelf at the safe house, right next to a nine-year-old Cosmo magazine and a Jehovah's Witness publication. She hadn't been reading Scripture systematically like Carl did, starting at the beginning and working his way through to Revelation. She usually just flipped around until something caught her eye. She'd spent a lot of time in Jeremiah lately.

"For I know the plans I have for you."

She was glad someone did. Drisklay would be here in an hour or two with more information, but right now all she knew was she was going to South Dakota. She'd spent a lot of time praying her new home wouldn't have as many mosquitoes as Glennallen. She also would prefer to work somewhere where she didn't have to change a dozen diapers a day.

"For I know the plans I have for you."

Lacy had already decided that once she got to her new home, she would find a church there. Maybe even work up the courage to join a Bible study or prayer group. She didn't want South Dakota to turn out like Alaska, where she only knew one or two casual acquaintances. No wonder she had felt so lonely there. Things had got a little easier once she met Kurtis, but …

She spent most of her waking hours trying not to think about him. She couldn't let her past life poison her future like she had before. She had come to Alaska still pining for Raphael, still mourning his loss, grieving to the point where she could never move on with her life. In South Dakota, she couldn't live another four years wishing for things that would never be. She remembered what her mom told her about breaking up with her doctor boyfriend. *He was an important part of my life for a season. We had fun memories.*

That's what Lacy wanted to hold onto when it came to her relationship with Kurtis. The memories. Memories of cuddling together on the couch while Madeline put on impromptu ballet shows. Of driving to Anchorage together, holding hands and enjoying the quietness of each other's company. Of helping Madeline build her very first snowman or take her first step on ice skates.

Those were good memories, and she was trying desperately not to sully them with the sorrow of this move. Sometimes things just didn't work out. It didn't mean Kurtis was a bad fit. It didn't mean the two of them weren't compatible. It just meant life had gotten in the way of what could have been.

In some ways, Lacy was glad to be starting over. Glad she didn't need the constant reminder of how foolish she'd been to waste four whole years agonizing over someone like Raphael. With him, it was easier to confine his memory to a distant point in the past. They had been good together back in Massachusetts, but everything after that had been a waste of energy at best. A nearly fatal mistake at worst. If only she had realized that sooner.

Sometimes she would look back and dissect those two and a half years she'd spent with Raphael. Were there signs? Could she have known what sort of jeopardy he'd drag her into, how much pain a few years of carefree spontaneity with him would cost? Lacy had finally begun to experience something new when it came to Raphael, something she had longed for during those four agonizing years in Glennallen.

Closure.

She couldn't change the past, couldn't take back those years they'd spent together travelling the East Coast in his Saab. She wasn't even sure she'd want to. Of course, she'd happily reverse time and never drive with him to the pier, but if Raphael was making such bad choices, they were bound to catch up to him eventually. It could have been worse. She could have been killed. Even if Raphael's contact hadn't gotten murdered that night in the North End, what would that mean? A life on the run with someone who offered fun and excitement but absolutely nothing by way of security.

He was an important part of my life for a season, Sandy had said. Her mom was so wise. Lacy hoped that she'd eventually learn to do the same thing with Kurtis. Move on. Accept the good times they'd had without wishing they could continue. With him, though, it was harder. Kurtis had never jeopardized her life, never cost her four years of pain and isolation. Still, she would have to go forward. She considered her placement in South Dakota God's way of giving her a new start. How many people would kill for a chance like that? Forget all the mistakes of the past, forget all the doomed relationships, the wasted time. A chance to start over with a clean record.

Lacy was trying to be grateful for that.

It was a start.

CHAPTER 27

"So here we have your identification."

Lacy took the card Drisklay handed her and stared at the picture, a close representation of herself on a South Dakota driver's license. *Marissa Hummel.* Well, it was better than Jo. Her birthday had changed. She was a year and a half older now. Fifteen pounds heavier. She hoped that wouldn't prove prophetic. She flipped the card around as if there would be more to discover about herself there.

"Birth certificate." Drisklay passed her the crisp page, and Lacy stared at the names of parents, dates, and cities she had never heard of. She'd have to get used to it. This was her life now.

"My folks made you a resume. I think you'll find you have a little more to work with than what we gave you last time."

Lacy's hands shook just a little as she held up the paper. Right there on top was an associate's degree dated three years ago. She doubted if whoever put it there would realize how vindicated it made her feel. Those community college credits she took in Massachusetts hadn't been completely wasted after all.

She scanned her employment history. Marissa Hummel had volunteered at an animal shelter since high school and then worked various retail jobs before moving to nowhere, South Dakota. "This would be great if I ever want to work at Petco."

Drisklay took a sip of coffee. "Good. You've got an interview there next week."

"Where? At Petco?"

He strummed his finger on his disposable cup. "I figured you could use a break from kids."

Lacy took a deep breath. It was a lot to take in. Of course, it was going to feel a little overwhelming. But she could get used to it. She was older now, more mature. There were worse jobs than working at a pet store, right? She had been reading in Philippians a few nights ago and came across a verse about complaining. *Do all things without complaining and disputing.* For the first time, Lacy experienced what Carl and Sandy and other Christians talked about, how reading the Bible could reveal your own sinfulness. It wasn't as pleasant or exciting as they all made it sound.

She thought back over the years she spent in Glennallen,

how she'd always found something to complain about. The weather, the mosquitoes, the daycare kids. She had grumbled incessantly about Drisklay and the witness protection program even though they were the ones who kept her alive.

She wasn't going to live like that until she withered up and died a bitter old woman. So what if Petco wasn't the future she'd pictured for herself? She couldn't change it. It wouldn't be easy starting over, but she could do it.

She hoped.

Drisklay handed her the rest of the small file. High school diploma. Childhood shots record. Last, he held up an unmarked envelope.

"What's this?" she asked.

He cleared his throat. "This is something my team and I have decided to leave up to you."

She wasn't sure she liked the way he was looking at her.

"Your assailants will be looking for a single woman, so we agreed we had to come up with a different cover."

He opened the envelope and handed her a slip of paper.

"Certificate of divorce?" Lacy read.

Drisklay nodded. "This guy, this Frank Bulgari, you married him right out of high school, divorced him a year and a half later. No contest. No kids. No baggage. Just a blip on the radar."

Lacy didn't want to touch the page. There was something else Drisklay wasn't telling her.

"That's option one." His fingers hesitated before he pulled out another form. "Here's option two." He passed her the document.

"A marriage license?" Lacy stared at it. "What, you're giving me an imaginary husband? I think people will eventually figure out that I'm not living with anybody."

"That's why we have a gentleman pre-screened and chosen for the job."

Lacy was sure she misheard him. Was this his way of making a joke? *Pre-screened?* He couldn't really think he could take two perfect strangers, bind them together with his forged marriage license and actually expect them to live together, could he?

She reached for the divorce paper. "Give me that one."

Drisklay chewed on his red coffee stirrer. "Before you make up your mind, maybe you want to meet your potential husband." He glanced at the document. "A certain Mr. Hank Murphy."

The name sounded like a sixty-year-old plumber. Not Lacy's idea of a romantic conquest.

"Mr. Murphy is a gym teacher at a private Christian school. Baseball, football ... You name it, he can coach it."

Lacy stared at the forged wedding certificate. "So you found this guy who's willing to marry a girl he's never met and ..."

"It's not quite that simple," Drisklay interrupted. "He's got experience that would allow him to offer certain protective services. And he's on the run too, you see. So in a way, hiding you two together would be a two-for-the-price-of-one deal from our end of things."

That's what this was all about? Lightening his paperwork load?

"I really don't think ..."

Drisklay pulled out one more envelope. "Before you make up your mind, take a look at the file we have on him."

She rolled her eyes but did as he requested. Hank Murphy's portfolio was about like hers. Birth certificate, college diploma, driver's license ... She pulled out his identification and squinted at the grainy photo. "Wait. Is that ...?"

One corner of Drisklay's lips curled up in an unsettling grin that looked completely out of place and unpracticed on his otherwise expressionless face. "I'd like to introduce you to your potential husband, Mr. Hank Murphy."

He turned his head and mumbled something into his hand-held radio.

The front door opened, followed by the pitter patter of excited, tiny feet rushing down the hall. "Daddy says you might be my new mommy!"

Lacy had already gotten down from her chair and knelt on the ground to catch Madeline, who ran with arms outstretched for a hug. Lacy nuzzled her face in Madeline's hair, surprised by the tear that was sneaking down her cheek.

"Daddy says the bad men who tried to shoot you are angry with him because he arrested one of their friends. He says we get to move to a whole new state, and if you say so, we can all move together and you and Daddy will be married, and I'll be your daughter, and I'm never allowed to say anything about Alaska because it's a really big secret and we don't want the bad guys finding out where we are, so it's kind of like hide and seek, and won't you please marry Daddy so we can all be a family?"

Lacy didn't know what to say. Was this some sort of trick? Drisklay's attempt at humor? She looked up at him, saw him hiding a wide smile behind his coffee cup.

Lacy rose to her feet. Kurtis stood behind his daughter, looking both shy and hopeful. "For the record," he said, "I voted against the big surprise entrance."

Lacy stared at him. Blinked her eyes to make sure all this was really happening. It had to be a dream.

He took a step forward. "Munchkin and I have to lay low one way or another." He brought his face closer to Lacy's and whispered, "We've already gotten two death threats, and I caught an intruder lurking around the daycare."

The acid in Lacy's stomach curdled. Someone had gone after Madeline?

"I called Drisklay, told him what was going on. Said I had to leave anyway, so why couldn't I leave with you? Help keep you safe and get the munchkin away from all the drama. I guess he thought it was a good idea." Kurtis took her hands in his. "I don't want to rush anything. If you're not ready, if you need more time to think about it ..."

Outside, a marching band played a slightly off-key rendition of *The Stars and Stripes Forever*.

Kurtis shifted his weight and took a small box out of his pocket. "But, well, I've already got this ring, and it *is* the Fourth of July ..."

He dropped to one knee and opened the case. Madeline was hanging on his arm, beaming as bright as Alaska's midnight sun.

"Marissa Hummel, will you be my wife?"

Madeline let go of her dad to wrap her arms around Lacy's leg. "Please?" she begged.

Lacy didn't know if she was doing more laughing or crying. "Yes," she answered. "Yes, I will."

Kurtis slipped on the ring. It was a perfect fit.

Madeline bounced up and down, clapping her hands. "Goody, goody, goody!"

Drisklay cleared his throat. "We better get down to business if we want to have you three in South Dakota by tonight."

More music from the parade floated by. Kurtis and Lacy sat down in front of the pile of documents. Drisklay stirred his empty coffee cup. "So now that we've settled on that, let's talk about your new life."

FROM ALANA TERRY:

Identity Theft was the first book I wrote after moving from Anchorage to a small Alaska community of about 400. It wasn't until I went back and re-read this story about a city girl struggling to adapt to rural living that I realized how autobiographical it really was.

(Yes, that was a somewhat embarrassing realization!)

I learned to love rural Alaska, however even in spite of the inherent danger of living so far away from conventional medical care! I'll tell you all about my multiple experiences on med-evac planes and jets, but first... more suspense (the fictional kind this time).

Would you remain in an abusive home situation if that was the only you had to protect someone you loved? Kimmie is old enough to leave home and now that her mother's died, she doesn't have to stay trapped under her step dad's oppressive rule.

She wants nothing more than to be free... but can she abandon her little brother to her step-dad's abusive tyranny?

Termination Dust is another Alaskan Refuge Christian suspense novel. If you like gritty, fast-paced thrills, this story will not disappoint.

Readers are calling it "astounding," "gritty," and "unforgettable," and you can dive right into this heart-pounding suspense novel now.

Read *Termination Dust* today.

Can you handle the cold?